CONTACT CARDS

CONTACT CARDS

An Extraterrestrial Divination System

KIM CARLSBERG & DARRYL ANKA

ILLUSTRATED BY

DARRYL ANKA

BEAR & COMPANY
PUBLISHING
SANTA FE, NEW MEXICO

LIBRARY OF CONGRESS CATALOGING-IN-PUBLICATION DATA

Carlsberg, Kim, 1955–
    Contact cards : an extraterrestrial divination system / Kim
    Carlsberg & Darryl Anka : illustrated by Darryl Anka.
        p. cm.
    Includes bibliographical references.
    ISBN 1-879181-32-0
        1. Life on other planets—Miscellanea. 2. Fortune-telling by cards.
I. Anka, Darryl, 1951– . II. Title.
BF1779.L5C37 1996   96-1375
133.3'242—dc20   CIP

Bear & Company
Santa Fe, NM 87504-2860

Card and Book Illustrations: Darryl Anka

Interior and Package Design: Marilyn Hager

Editing: Barbara Doern Drew

Typography: Marilyn Hager

Printed in the United States by RR Donnelley & Sons

2 4 6 8 9 7 5 3 1

It is with profound love and appreciation that we dedicate this divination system to our one and only spaceship Earth. May her inhabitants pilot her with resounding respect into a healthy and harmonious future.

CONTENTS

ACKNOWLEDGMENTS

We would like to thank Barbara Hand Clow, Gerry Clow, and the wonderful staff of Bear & Company for distributing the power and truth of extraterrestrial contact through the publishing of *Contact Cards: An Extraterrestrial Divination System*.

We would also like to give special thanks to Barbara Hand Clow for the critical contribution made in the specific Contact Card Chiron. Through her groundbreaking book *Chiron: Rainbow Bridge Between the Inner and Outer Planets*, we were able to establish and utilize the essential energy of this recently discovered minor planet to good effect in the completion of this divination system.

Finally, we would like to thank the extraterrestrials for their transformative contact and inspiration in the creation of this deck.

PREFACE

This unique tool for growth, *Contact Cards: An Extraterrestrial Divination System*, is the result of many years of investigation and experience with the standard tarot, other divination systems, the subject of UFOs, and the exploration of spiritual energy in its various expressions.

However, this knowledge was accumulated not only through research, but through firsthand involvement as well. Kim Carlsberg has the dubious honor of participating in ongoing contacts with extraterrestrial "visitors" in a form of human/alien interaction that has come to be known as "abduction." Through innumerable contacts over her lifetime, she has amassed a great deal of knowledge concerning the aliens, other-dimensional realms, and the higher energies employed in the aliens' technology.

In addition, through these experiences Kim has gained a new perspective on the beauty and wonders of life, nature, and the environment right here on planet Earth. This divination system was an inspiration born of her growing ability to perceive all life as "one" and her recognition that each being, be it human, animal, tree, stone, or alien, is a symbolic aspect and reflection in its own way of all other forms in creation.

Darryl Anka was inspired to begin researching UFOs after two close-range, broad-daylight sightings in 1973. In each case, the UFO was a dark, metallic, triangular craft about thirty feet on each side.

Both sightings were witnessed by friends who were with him at those times, and each lasted for at least a full minute. In the first instance, the craft glided smoothly away over the horizon; the second ship accelerated straight up in an instant.

Eventually, Darryl's research led him to accumulate knowledge on metaphysical subjects such as channeling. After further study, he became a practicing channel for an extraterrestrial consciousness known as "Bashar," whose teachings focus on the nature of consciousness and reality and how each person can learn to manifest a more creative and joyful life. Additionally, Darryl learned the traditional tarot and has given readings since 1972.

Kim and Darryl's first project together was a book about Kim's alien abduction experiences, *Beyond My Wildest Dreams: Diary of a UFO Abductee*. The book was authored by Kim and illustrated by Darryl, who has also been a special-effects illustrator in the film industry. It was published by Bear & Company in the fall of 1995.

Contact Cards: An Extraterrestrial Divination System seemed like the next logical project through which to express their mutual interest in increasing public awareness concerning the multifaceted phenomenon known as alien contact. These encounter experiences are becoming more prevalent in our society and are providing new opportunities for personal transformation now and into the future.

PART ONE
THE SYSTEM

INTRODUCTION

It can be said that the universe is divided into two separate aspects: the visible and the invisible. We can perceive the rocks and trees around us, but we cannot see the gravity that keeps everything firmly in place. We have done a fair job of creating scientific devices that allow us to detect some of these invisible energies, such as ultraviolet light, x-rays, and other forms of electromagnetic radiation, but the majority of the cosmos still remains undetectable by us.

The exterior universe is not the only thing that is composed of visible and invisible elements. Humans, and perhaps all living creatures, are a combination of both visible physical "hardware"—our bodies—and invisible energetic "software"—our minds or consciousnesses.

Like gravity, our minds have a very real effect in the physical world. Yet no one has been able to pin down just exactly what or where the mind is, nor where it comes from. Is the mind—that is, our ability to think, imagine, intuit, and create—simply a side effect of the physical brain's electrochemical activity? Or, as many people believe, does the mind result when pure nonphysical consciousness projects itself into physical form, as in the concept of spiritual incarnation?

Regardless of the answer, many of us possess a curiosity to know more about our invisible inner selves. To that end, several tools have been created over the course of human history to help us map the hidden terrain of our conscious, subconscious, and unconscious realms, just as telescopes and space probes have helped us to map the heavens.

Psychology is one such tool. However, like any device, its ability to discover new information is limited by one major factor: It was designed by people who had a preconceived idea of what they wanted the tool to find. Thus, the tool can only "reveal" what it was created to find—the original preconceived notion. Unfortunately, many people using such disciplinary tools often believe that once the tool has revealed a specific answer to a question, there are no other answers that can apply. This is not to say that psychology is without merit. When used with sensitivity and intuition, it can bring about penetrating insights into the nature of the human mind.

During the years we have spent researching UFOs and extraterrestrial contact, it has become clear that the phenomenon is not limited to the visible, physical universe. There are strong indications that alien contact, in the form of telepathic communication, may also be taking place within the deep levels of our intangible consciousnesses.

It is for this reason, and because humans are now beginning to realize we are not alone in the universe, that we feel the timing is appropriate for a new tool: *Contact Cards: An Extraterrestrial Divination System.*

Tools such as tarot cards and other oracular—or divination—systems are usually the products of the intuitive, creative level of our minds. The advantage to this is that the subconscious mind has been used to create a tool that speaks directly in the language of the subconscious: pictographic symbols.

We all know that when we are visiting a foreign country, if we have learned to speak the local language we get a much deeper, more complex, and richer understanding of the culture than if we rely upon a stilted, literal translation in our native tongue. In the country of the subconscious mind, a single picture is truly worth a thousand words.

With this in mind (so to speak), we believe that the images contained in *Contact Cards* will speak directly to the subconscious minds of the seeker and the reader. They will therefore assist in revealing the inner-realm dialogues that we believe already may be happening between the subconscious minds within humanity and the corresponding mental levels within extraterrestrial intelligences.

To complement the artistic nature of the cards and to reinforce the symbolic approach required to more easily access the subconscious mind of the seeker, each Contact Card has been given a story to help define its unique energetic quality. Each suit has also been given its own style of story so that the conscious mind will not become too familiar with how the information is delivered and start to fall back on preconceived notions. This way, the reader's intuition is always engaged and is free to interpret each card as it sees fit.

We believe that everyone possesses some connection to extraterrestrial energy, since everything in the universe is part of the One. However, we would like to remind the reader and/or the seeker using this divination tool to apply the connections and guidance he or she might discover to his or her life on Earth. In this way, we remain grounded rather than assuming that all life's challenges will be solved by "escaping" to the stars.

Suits

Contact Cards: An Extraterrestrial Divination System has been designed to contain five different suits: Aliens, Ships, Stars, Planets, and Crop Circles. There are twelve cards in each suit, totaling sixty cards.

Though each card symbolizes a unique quality, these five suits were chosen because of how they reflect the archetypal elements of a spiritual quest:

- Aliens represent the person who is seeking knowledge.

- Ships reflect the "vehicle"—that is, the style of expression or personal behavior—the seeker uses on his or her journey through life.

- Stars illuminate the energy of the goal, outcome, and transformation the seeker desires.

- Planets represent the situation or environment in which the seeker finds himself or herself at present.

- Crop Circles symbolize the advice, messages, and guidance available to the seeker.

These designations do not mean that the suits specifically represent these qualities in every reading—only that they lend these energy traits to the reading as a whole. In other words, the suits form a kind of underlying template or foundation for each reading.

The deck functions holographically in that this template provides continuity and clarity for each individual card as well as for each spread of cards. Therefore, in the five-card spread, for example, where positions one through five represent the five archetypal elements (see "Layouts"), those positions can be filled with any card, rather than with cards from only a single suit.

The Aliens and Ships that were chosen for this divination system were picked from a wide range of reported contacts and UFO sightings. Though many types of beings and crafts have been seen, we narrowed our selections to those we believe are most intimately involved with humanity's evolution and spiritual growth at the present time. This belief is based on reports of spiritual acceleration and expanded knowledge concerning the nature of consciousness as a direct result of such contacts.

Choosing the Stars and Planets was more straightforward. The planets of our solar system have long been associated with various energies and archetypal symbols through the practice of astrology. We felt it was appropriate to continue that tradition. At the same time, we wanted to acknowledge how the science of astronomy has expanded our awareness of the amazing variety of stellar phenomena that fills the heavens—interesting and unusual star systems that unknown alien civilizations may call home.

Crop Circles represent one of the strangest occurrences unfolding on Earth, though most people are still unaware that they exist. Huge geometric designs have been appearing for years—possibly hundreds of years—in the crop fields of farmers around the world, but primarily in the fields of England near sacred sites like Stonehenge.

Stalks of wheat, barley, and other grains are laid down—bent and flattened—into ornate patterns by some mysterious force. These "agriglyphs," as they are sometimes called, are always formed in the dark of night and in a matter of only minutes, even though many of these crop circle patterns are hundreds of feet across and mathematically complex.

There have been sightings of unusual lights in the sky prior to the formation of many of the circles. It still remains a speculation, UFO theories aside, as to what these lights might be and whether they are connected to the creation of the crop patterns.

Despite a few verified hoaxes and claims by some people that they are responsible for creating the glyphs, thousands of genuine crop circles have exhibited characteristics, such as cell-structure mutation in the wheat stalks, that are beyond the capabilities of human technology. As such, the crop circle phenomenon remains a genuine mystery.

Shadow Qualities

Many divination systems, such as the traditional tarot, incorporate the concept of a "shadow side" to each of the cards—a polarized, opposing, and usually negative energy that represents the dark side of each positive symbol. Often, this shadow quality is reflected when a card is drawn in an upside-down position.

Because light and dark energies are inherent in all situations in life, we have blended the positive (light) and negative (shadow) qualities of each Contact Card within its respective definition. There is no upside-down position to the Contact Cards, and no distinct line is drawn between what represents either a positive or a negative layout of the cards. It is up to the reader of the cards to use his or her discernment and psychic sensitivity in determining how the light or shadow attributes apply in any given reading.

Finally, to reinforce the light and dark aspects of each card equally, the central images have been rendered in black and white.

LAYOUTS

There are five recommended ways to read Contact Cards, as illustrated in the spreads on the following page. However, experienced tarot and divination-system practitioners may wish to experiment using this deck in other configurations to gain more detailed insights or simply because other methods are more familiar or preferred. The layouts consist of the following: one-, three-, five-, seven-, and nine-card spreads.

Insight

The first method is the single-card draw. This spread is helpful when the seeker desires a quick insight or an illuminating energy that defines the now moment or the outcome most likely to manifest from present circumstances.

Triad

The second method consists of three cards laid out in a triangle. The first card symbolizes the challenge at hand, the second card calls upon the message of guidance, and the third card signifies the probable outcome if the guidance is followed.

Pentagram

The third method is a spread of five cards. This is the standard spread for Contact Cards, as each position perfectly mirrors the energies of the five suits. The cards are laid in a crosslike spiral-galaxy formation proceeding from the left through the bottom, middle, and top to the final position on the right.

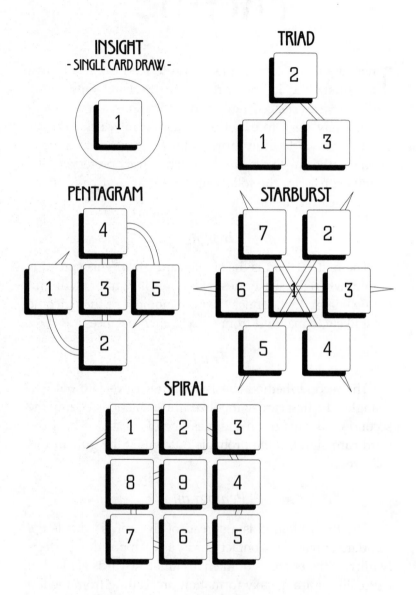

Sample Layout Spreads

As in general with the suits, these five positions now specifically represent (1) the seeker and his or her hopes, fears, and goals; (2) the conditions, circumstances, and other formative factors involved in why the seeker is asking for insight; (3) any messages from guides or from within the seeker's life that may be invisible; (4) the process or journey required to create the seeker's desired outcome; and (5) the most likely outcome based on the seeker's present energy and willingness to incorporate the guiding messages. If the final card does not produce the desired result, it will contain insights as to what direction the seeker must explore in order to get on track.

Starburst

The fourth method is a spread of seven cards. These are laid out like a starburst, with the initial card in the center and the remaining six surrounding it in a clockwise circle, beginning in the two o'clock position.

This spread delves into more explicit details, once again beginning with (1) the challenge, question, or circumstances at hand. It then moves through and explores (2) the seeker's beliefs and definitions of life that have manifested the present conditions; (3) the seeker's emotional tapestry that results from the foundational beliefs and thus can be used to illuminate what type of definitions may be causing the emotional patterns; (4) the thought patterns that define the seeker's choices in life; and (5) the actions that are the behavior that extends from the seeker's beliefs, emotions, and thoughts.

Card 6 has a powerful role in this spread. It illuminates the best process or energy state necessary to understand the four foundational patterns currently in force and to alter each one in a way that will produce (7) the desired outcome if these adjustments are attended to.

If the seeker is unwilling to process and transform the information revealed in this spread, it will show in the outcome card, as the hoped-for result will not manifest. Instead, the final position will indicate what will happen if the seeker does not rise to the challenge of exploring and transforming his or her template energies.

Spiral

The fifth spread contains nine cards laid out consecutively in three rows of three. By their order they mirror the energy of a "creation spiral," an ancient symbol known to many native cultures and representing the creative force in nature.

These positions signify (1) the desired goal; (2) the strongest fear of the seeker; (3) the immediate obstacles created by this fear; (4) the lessons to be learned by turning the obstacles into opportunities; (5) the best process by which the seeker can begin this transformation; (6) the insights that can be gained on this journey; (7) the intention that must be present for success; (8) the actions necessary to be in alignment with the intention; and (9) the outcome of adhering to the advice, or the shadow result of moving ahead before the seeker has accomplished the inner work suggested by the spread.

PART TWO:
THE CARDS

ALIENS

CARD	ATTRIBUTE
Android	Patterns
Anunnaki	Origin
Arcturus	Archetype
Association	Council
Hybrid	Balance
Lyra	Parent
Mantis	Persistence
Orion	Control
Pleiades	Passion
Reptilian	Shadow
Sirius	Play
Zeta	Intellect

ALIENS

Each alien card represents a different energy dynamic, symbolic not only of the various extraterrestrial cultures depicted, but also of the corresponding qualities expressed in humanity. All of the alien types shown in Contact Cards are modeled after beings that have been reported by many people during the past several decades either as face-to-face contacts, astral encounters, or telepathic communications.

In such cases where an extraterrestrial was said to be a higher-dimensional, nonphysical being, a graphic representation has been created for this system according to the quality of the energy or personality perceived. In the case of Sirius, a dolphin acts as an additional symbol since it is believed that dolphins may be in telepathic contact with Sirian consciousness. They also represent a nonhuman intelligence cohabitating Earth.

All alien symbols depicted in the border of each Alien card are authentic as reported by eyewitness accounts.

ANDROID

Android, automaton,
little wind-up doll,
worker drone—
no thoughts of your own,
no order is too tall.
The same routine day after day . . .
what kind of life is this?
Is it true what they say,
that ignorance is bliss?

Every day is the same schedule, the android thought,
which was fine with him because that's all he knew. *Time
to go to work now, time to go to work.*

The android followed the same route he always took
through the flying saucer factory, where many other
androids like himself hand-built beautiful spaceships that
were famous throughout the universe for their precision.
But he didn't notice their beauty because his only job was to
notice whether they measured up to specifications.

From time to time, as the android fulfilled his task,
checking this, inspecting that, he would overhear the
Masters telling tales of the fantastic places that they had discovered while journeying in these ships. However, the
android could not appreciate the magic of faraway worlds
and exotic beings that were experienced by the Masters. He
had to measure the width of the seams on the antigravity
generator casings; they had to be just right.

Over the course of his life, the android had overheard
many stories of passion and glory, pain and sacrifice, and

the rise and fall of great empires—enough to fill the memory banks of many androids. Since these powerful and emotional adventures were nothing more than bits of information that did not assist him in making more precise measurements, he erased them at the end of every shift without a second thought.

In spite of centuries of loyal service, however, one day the Masters replaced the android with their crowning achievement: model #20002. There were no good-byes, no recognitions of his flawless record—just a short ride to the recycling center.

As he was being disassembled, the android reflected on all that had happened to him. *I've inspected 4,000,532 generator casing seams to within 1/5000th of an angstrom*, he thought. *I wonder if I missed anything?*

The Android card reminds us that it is very easy—indeed, automatic—for us to become stuck in the humdrum mode of materialism and survival.

We must not allow the tendency of Western society to overproduce and to concentrate entirely on end results to keep us in straits. By embracing the present, by being in the eternal now and not focusing too strongly on our accomplishments, we will be able to hear the whispers life is constantly sending our way.

When we surrender to the knowledge that we are always supported abundantly, Spirit provides us with synchronistic shortcuts to obtaining our goals. If we are too narrowly focused, we will be closed off to these gifts and, additionally, we will miss the precious nuances of day-to-day living.

We must learn to be precise and give attention to detail, but not to the exclusion of the overall picture. In other words, we must take time to enjoy the path as well as the goal, for they are really one and the same.

This card instructs us that in order to express our full potential, we must go beyond the limitations of our programming. We should constantly stretch by examining our beliefs, feelings, and behavior.

This way, we interact from moment to moment with the rich emotional tapestry of our humanity instead of mundanely reacting from conditioning. Survival patterns, originally taught to us in childhood in order to protect us from real harm, can persist long after they are useful, creating resistance to new experiences.

A life without curiosity, introspection, and motivation to change becomes blocked and stagnant. This card cautions us not to be like the android and find at the end of our days that we have been isolated by our limited programming from the magic life has to offer. The message of the android is to get out of our ruts—to do something different and to think in new ways.

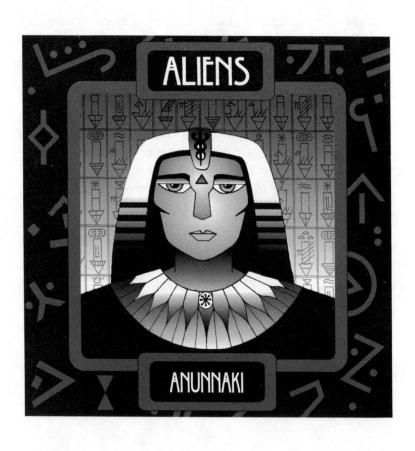

ANUNNAKI

Bedazzled by an auric glow,
the gods of old did make a plan
to take their seeds to Earth and sow,
until their harvest begat man.

The humans, male and female, toiled
upon Earth both day and night.
With clay and blood, they were soiled
until they woke and saw the light.

From that day forth, men claimed Earth
and gods withdrew on high.
Mankind learned its own worth
and now reaches for the sky.

In the beginning, after the creator gods from Lyra had been manifest as physical beings for countless millennia, they began to notice that their once thousand-year life spans were dwindling to a mere few centuries. With so much beauty yet to be experienced in the physical worlds, all were dismayed to find deterioration accelerating with each new generation.

They decided to devote all available resources toward solving this problem and finally, after many years, discovered a magic elixir made from gold. By drinking this divine fluid, their precious corporeal forms regenerated and regained their treasured thousand-year vitality.

Realizing that the amount of gold on their home world wouldn't last forever, the creator gods chose to search for more worlds rich in the yellow metal and they eventually landed upon the ancient Earth. This planet was abundant in the remarkable ore, and the creator beings mined the soil with vigor for several hundred thousand years. Over time, they tired of this task but were unwilling to give up for fear degeneration would reoccur.

One among them, a brilliant scientist, had a plan. She suggested that by infusing their own humanoid DNA into Earth's indigenous ape creatures, a new hybrid race of workers could be cultivated to mine the gold in their stead.

The plan was a success, and the creator gods were excited at the degree to which the engineered species favored their physiology. The demigods taught the newly spawned Earth humans how to speak, how to work, and how to grow food to sustain themselves. What the creators didn't expect, however, was that their human workers would also learn to think for themselves.

After generations of servitude spent quenching their creators' thirst for the golden elixir, the evolving humans yearned for sovereignty. They also began to understand the purpose and power of the fruits of their labor. Naturally, they desired the life-giving liquid for themselves, and they eventually beseeched Anu, the leader of their masters, for equal consideration and treatment.

Anu's compassion for the humans prompted him to hold council with his followers to discuss the dilemma. These masters, whom the humans called Anunnaki, found themselves split in their beliefs for the first time. Some championed the humans, while the others feared there would not be enough gold to go around if humans were given the gift of longevity.

Finally, the leader of all the creator beings came to a decision. "Did we not make these humans in our image, after our kind? They are our children and have developed in a way that must be respected. These children have earned their right to live freely. Let us leave them in peace."

So the Anunnaki left Earth in the care of the humans but retained the secret of transforming gold into extended life. From that day forward, the humans have worshiped their golden god, feverishly seeking to rediscover the mysterious fountain of youth their creators kept for themselves.

The Anunnaki card puts us in touch with our individual and collective origins. It represents the first moment of creation of any undertaking.

The Anunnaki energy is steeped in ancient knowledge and forms the template or blueprint upon which all our activities are based. We are reminded to examine the foundation of the current situation—in other words, what brought us to this moment, what was the original cause that ultimately resulted in the present experience.

The shadow side of this card warns that if the initial ingredients are not harmonious, not inclusive of the ethical qualities of respect and equality, then our endeavors may fall apart and our lofty goals elude us. It also cautions us to be aware of those portions of our work and our personal lives that are rote and based on old programming and control patterns rather than original creativity.

An unharmonious beginning could also create difficult repercussions that may take a long time to correct. The counsel here is to "look before you leap," an "ounce of prevention" being worth the proverbial "pound of cure." On the other hand, if we have been mindful that everything is in its proper place before we set our desires in motion, then the dreams to which we give birth will have enduring qualities and long-lasting impact.

The Anunnaki card is also symbolic of the search for meaning in our lives: our personal purpose, our special service, and the awakening of our inner godhood.

If we take action upon our visions from within the golden light of unconditional love and respect, our manifestations will grow deep roots and expand toward the heavens, transforming all opponents into allies whether they intend to assist us or not.

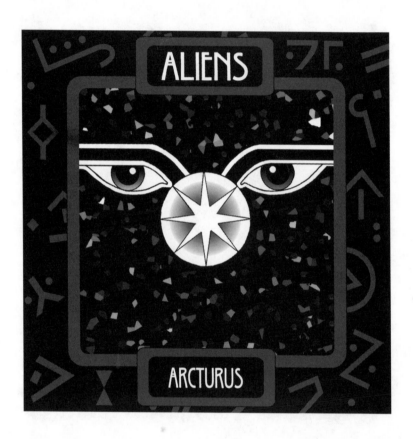

ARCTURUS

A reassuring whisper
gives us strength to carry on;
a little flame that lights our way,
from dusk until the dawn.

A steadfast friend,
always near when we feel alone,
gifting us with a guardian
angel all our own.

The small spirit seemed to be floating in a vast sparkling sea of warmth. *Where have all my friends gone?* he wondered. *They were here a moment ago.*

"Do not worry," a caressing voice resounded from everywhere at once. "You are not alone."

"Who are you," the little spirit asked, "and where am I?"

"You are floating within our consciousness," answered the voice. "You are immersed within our love."

"It feels wonderful," the spirit said, "but why can't I see you?"

"We are pure energy, pure being. Our thoughts support you . . . our caring sustains you . . . our intention guides you."

The little spirit was suddenly awash in a tingling wave of curiosity. "Guiding me where?"

"Toward a new experience where you are needed."

"Who is it who needs me?" The spirit vibrated, barely able to contain his excitement.

"Billions of beings," the voice informed him. "They are in desperate need of your light and your joy."

"How will I get there? Are they far?" the spirit wanted to know.

"You will pass through the star gate, one of the interdimensional doorways that are all around you, for we are Arcturus, the preparer of the way. Those who are in need of your help are waiting on the other side. Though you may not remember us when you arrive there, we will always be with you as your guides."

The little spirit felt a terrific compression, as though existence had collapsed within his soul. Darkness enveloped him, and he fell down a long tunnel toward a distant blinding light. Suddenly the light exploded all around him, and he was bombarded by a hundred sensations at once. He felt extremely heavy, and it was very hard to think. Everything was a blur.

Slowly, as his vision cleared, the spirit found himself looking into a pair of bright and hopeful eyes: deep, dark, moist eyes brimming with love just for him. And, strangely, he somehow knew he loved this being, too. As he gazed into those pools of compassion, he heard a new voice somewhere above him say, "Congratulations! It's a boy!"

To open the Arcturus gate is to invite angelic assistance and guidance into our lives. This archetypal energy summons us to service and to prepare for great life journeys.

This card speaks of the "little voice" within that helps us remain aligned with our truth and allows us to view life from a child's open and trusting perspective.

This is not to say that we should allow ourselves to be taken advantage of through naiveté. Our challenge is to transform vulnerability, which is the willingness to be open to the choices the universe offers us, into strength by belief in our unique talents and gifts. Such a perspective would also make it possible for us to see the world in new ways, for fresh opportunities are invisible to us until we accept their existence within our personal realities.

Arcturus indicates a high degree of connection to the etheric realms, which brings the opportunity for emotional healing, rejuvenation, and accessing the collective-conscious level of universal information known as the Akashic Records. With this energy at hand, we can always be assured that loving guidance is by our side all the days of our lives.

ASSOCIATION

Wise ones robed in
iron virtue
call for unity
from silken hearts—
separate minds of common purpose,
reaching out for peace.

General Meeting of the Association of Worlds
Star date 20053-1

Will the general assembly please come to order! Today, we are honored to receive into our association a new member world. As we all know, it is a great distinction for any planet to be recognized by the alliance, and it is a proud statement about the quality of life and the level of consciousness that the civilization has achieved.

It is important for this new member world to realize the responsibility that comes with fellowship. First and foremost is the commitment to be a shining example and guiding influence for other worlds in all stages of evolution.

The elders of this congregation are the greatest minds and most compassionate souls in the galaxy. Although it is an ongoing challenge to recognize, understand, and honor the diversity of all species, the elders serve as a constant reminder that the qualities of patience and love are the links that will eventually unite all worlds in peace.

Though it is the policy of the organization to be the big brother to all worlds, we will not openly interfere with the natural progression of any planet. We will, however, make sure that each request for assistance is answered in the appropriate manner for the stage of evolution of that society.

Now that the general outline of this assemblage has been expressed, we ask that the representatives of the new member world, Earth, please stand and recite the league's oath with us:

> We, the members of the Association of Worlds, do solemnly swear to uphold the standards and guidelines of the organization to our fullest abilities. As members, it is our duty to live and inspire others to live in truth and peace and with absolute respect for all forms of life. As members, we graciously give ourselves to the service of others and thankfully accept all opportunities to aid fellow travelers, recognizing one as all and all as one.

Congratulations to Earth for becoming the 4431st member of the Association of Worlds. We are ecstatic that you finally made it! Meeting adjourned.

This card is a recognition and a celebration that we have achieved a highly evolved level of spirituality. A pat on the back would be appropriate. Acceptance into the Association is a statement that we have successfully refined the ego and arrived at a place of harmony in our deepest core. It is also a reminder that all is one and that the truest expression of that idea is the commitment to be of service to others.

If the Association is holding council in our deck today, it is a call for communion with those who are like-minded. Any altruistic idea can be more easily manifested with the support of others maintaining the same goal. There is power in numbers, and the camaraderie we desire is likewise soliciting our partnership.

The possible catch to commingling with elitist company and becoming part of a privileged class is that this can give us a false sense of self. It is easy for our egos to identify with the reputation and merit of an individual or group with which we are associated and lead us to become puffed up or conceited. We should also be aware of the temptation to relinquish individual responsibility and hide behind or ride on the efforts of our associates.

The deepest essence of the Association card represents group energies and identifying our selves with the mass consciousness of a larger structure—external groups or the internal collective consciousness. It is indicative of a highly evolved state of being in which the ego constantly redefines itself, having more and more of the soul's perspective.

This type of psychological atmosphere results in the ability of probable, or alternate reality, selves and reincarnational past- or future-life selves to consciously communicate with one another. Sharing their combined knowledge and experience further adds to the creative expression of the whole.

On a more cosmic level, when an individual draws the Association card, it is the marker that he or she has acknowledged his or her multidimensionality. Such remarkable experiences as contact with extraterrestrial and extradimensional beings are now not only available, but a natural outgrowth of spiritual development.

Contact is not merely a matter of being at the right place at the right time. It is also a result of personal resonance: like attracts like. Contact comes from expanding the definition of self beyond that of an individualized ego. Once this concept has taken hold, the door to communication with extraterrestrials and extradimensionals opens.

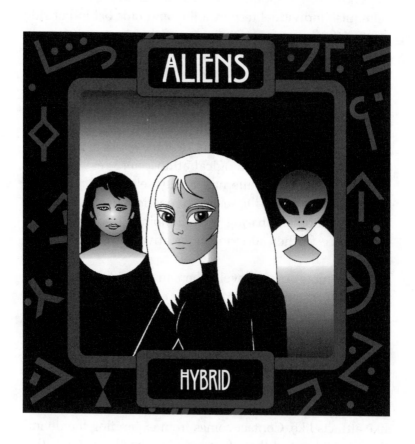

HYBRID

What am I to think
about these feelings?
What am I to feel
about these thoughts?
Do I go with my emotion,
or do I think everything through?
How do I determine
to which side I must be true?

One of my fathers leads me by the hand as always, but for the first time, I notice that I have more fingers than he. I turn to look at his familiar face, but I am aware, as never before, how much larger his eyes are than mine. He asks me how I am, but his lips never move. Today, I understand that we are different.

This makes me afraid. I feel empty inside; I have these feelings I know he has never been able to perceive. Today they are stronger than ever before.

In my mind, I rush to the place I visit in my dreams. I want to be there now—safe in the arms of the one who looks like me, the one who understands my feelings, the one who fills me with love. My father stops and listens to my thoughts more closely. Today, for some unknown reason he seems to comprehend my fear.

"Come," my father announces, and we enter a place I have never been before: the room of the "New Ones." He carries me past rows of tiny boxes. "These are your newest brothers and sisters," Father explains. They sleep soundly—hundreds of little babies of many different colors. As I count fingers and toes I notice that some of them look like Father, but more of them look like me.

Where do we come from, and why are we all so different? So many questions fill my mind I become dizzy and confused. Father observes my thoughts with heightened concentration. He merges his consciousness with mine to better understand, but as much as he desires to, with all his mental power he cannot feel my emotions.

He hastily directs me to another room that has always been private. A vibration surrounds us, and I am lost in a sea of blackness. Memories ebb and flow through me— memories of the one in my dreams. My questions are answered as quickly as they form. I see a planet with a blue atmosphere, clouds swirling round and round. There are millions of others like myself all sharing emotion, but not sharing thought. . . . How strange!

But something is terribly wrong. Due to ignorant choices made by these people called humans, their planet is polluted and dying. I understand that I cannot be with those whom I am most like because I would be in danger there.

Although I feel sad about this probable future of the planet called Earth, I see how fortunate I am to be the first of a new species: one that will combine the power of emotion with the wisdom required to explore its potential without being controlled by it. Time and space pulsate through me; I am anxious but excited. My father is beside me . . . observing. It is obvious that we are taking a trip!

The motion slows. My heart beats in anticipation. A moment later a door appears in the darkness, and we enter a room filled with adult humans and other children like me. I am instantly flooded with all the joy in the universe at once, as my eyes fall upon the one in my dreams.

"This is your mother," Father whispers.

The hybrid being on this card is the result of meticulous genetic manipulation, whereby the best attributes of two dissimilar species are blended to produce a whole new possibility in creation. This is one of the most powerful and positive Contact Cards, as it represents new beginnings with inherent balance and infinite possibilities for fulfillment, both psychological and emotional.

If we are in a state of confusion about our identity and/or purpose in life when we draw the Hybrid, it is a reassuring rejoinder that we are about to enter a new phase of self-discovery. We are about to uncap the latent potential we possess in the gift of our carefully nurtured genetic codes.

As the hybrid in the preceding story is the biological bridge between emotion and intellect, this card is an indication that we are about to merge opposite energies or ideas that have long been at odds. The child of this union will be harmony.

However, if this opportunity is ignored or we fail to govern our feelings during these sometimes confusing periods of growth, there is the possibility that the results may be irreparable. Emotion is a unique quality not native to all sentient beings. It is our responsibility to appreciate its exceptional nature and use it in tandem with our intelligence. Balance is the beat in the heart of success.

LYRA

Lyra, ancient mother,
your legends lost to time eternal—
with infinity between us,
would you recognize me?

In a remote section of the galaxy, a small gathering of celestial creator gods had an inspiration: "What would it be like to walk upon the surface of these wondrous worlds the Infinite has fashioned?" Excitement rippled through the group, and they set about to fulfill this fantastic idea. "The perfect vehicles for us should have feet to run through the fields, hands to hold each other, eyes to marvel at the endless sunsets, and ears to hear the songs of the wind."

After aeons of contemplation and preparation, a miracle became manifest. These architects of form melded their spirits with the primal elements of a remote planet orbiting the brilliant star of Lyra. The human body took form out of the intensity of their desire, appearing as two complements, male and female—the first mother and father.

Thus, the human race was born in the Lyran system. As they evolved, these newly created beings would eventually scatter their seeds throughout the galaxy.

The Lyrans were a beautiful, spiritual people whose technological achievements allowed them to traverse the heavens. Their encounters with beings of foreign worlds added a rich diversity to their own culture.

But the polarized nature of matter versus spirit also expanded, giving rise to conflict and generations of war on their home world. Finding no way to resolve their conflict, factions of their population split off, seeking refuge in other star systems, such as the Pleiades, Orion, Sirius, and Sol, which contains the planet Earth, in order to start over.

Sirius and the Pleiades were finally successful in achieving harmony. Others, such as in the Orion system and on Earth, continue to struggle toward the light.

To draw the card of Lyra is to draw on the mother and father within us all. This energy focuses on parenting, family, and inheritance in all forms: love, information, and patterns of belief and behavior.

Lyra expresses the value of knowledge that has passed through generations. She points out how deeper understanding of ourselves and the nature of reality can be gleaned through the teachings of the great masters, whether they are revered spiritual leaders or our own ancestors.

The shadow side of this idea tells us to be careful not to continue antiquated concepts of thought and action just because "that's the way it's always been" or because our attempt to grow in a different direction may require uncomfortable adjustments.

If we have a problem and we have inherited the card of Lyra this day, she suggests that this is not the time to react emotionally from the inner child or to feel the need to carry the burden of important decisions by ourselves. This is the time, as discerning adults, to listen to the voice of the parent within and/or to literally ask the advice of a parent or respected authority. We will best benefit by relying on the qualities that maturity and experience provide before acting.

On the other hand, it is equally critical to choose our own paths, to be conscious of balancing our male (assertive) and female (receptive) polarities, and to be cautious not to repeat the mistakes of the past. If existing conflicts are denying resolution, the best solution at this point is to break away completely and focus our energies in an entirely new direction.

In the realm of the physical, we should extend added appreciation for the miracle of our human bodies, and if there has been a longing, now is the perfect time to unfold the gift of life to other souls through the context of family. The Lyra card could also be reminding us not to ignore our already existing loved ones. We may need to give them a little extra affection and attention and to take special note of matters pertaining to family legacy, history, or inheritance.

In the realm of mind, there is fertile soil for planting new ideas at this time. We should imitate the creator gods in laying the foundation for monumental achievements and growth by adding new aspects to already existing ideas and forms.

It is also part of our Lyran heritage that we are travelers. Thus when distant lands call us to adventure beyond our familiar boundaries, we owe it to ourselves to go.

MANTIS

The die is cast,
the stage is set,
the tide cannot be turned.
Forget the past,
do not regret
the bridges you have burned.
Move forward now,
do not look back,
it's all so crystal clear.
The time is now,
stay right on track,
the place to be is here.

All lower-cast members immediately swoon down into postures of servitude as a skeletal frame regally enters the spacecraft's laboratory. While "Mantis" glides across the room emanating dominance with every breath, no one dares to question its authority, for this would be as fruitless as questioning reality itself. Mantis is omnipotent. It has always been and always will be. It has no enemies for it was the creator of creaturehood itself. Therefore, all abide without objection.

Mantis's frail arms dangle loosely. Its wiry appendages will never labor, for all jobs are performed by Mantis's loyal and obedient work force. These docile drones operate with independent bodies but are governed exclusively by Mantis's mental authority. Though capable and compliant, they are merely physical extremities of its vast hive mind.

The workers, as well as the spacecraft that carries them,

reflect the razor precision of Mantis's own psyche. Sleek, purely functional, and highly efficient, they approach their task with single-mindedness. Their sole purpose is to detain sentient beings and feed the insatiable mental appetite of their maker. For this is how Mantis sustains itself: feasting on the experiences and emotions of the species it cultivates.

Through the windows of the soul, Mantis enters with determination and skill. Bulging, glistening eyes penetrate the minds of its captives, searching for vicarious satisfaction, persisting until the deepest level of the unconscious delivers up its secrets. Eventually, the squirming detainees are returned to their native environments with no memory of the voyeur of their secret dreams.

The Mantis card carries an edge. With its razor-sharp intellect, Mantis forces us to focus on the issue at hand, bringing to bear all the resources, skills, and knowledge at our disposal.

We are urged to gather all our separate attributes into a single intense surge of energy that absorbs all seeming obstacles, adding their considerable inertia to its own relentless forward motion. Mantis instills us with the confidence and conviction that persistence will eventually wear down all blocks and drive the present circumstances toward inexorable evolutionary change.

If there is a secret to be gained from contact with Mantis, it is to walk the walk and talk the talk. If we give no reason for our authority to be questioned, it will most likely go unchallenged. Mantis epitomizes the concept that "attitude is everything!"

As always, however, there is a shadow side to this confidence. In walking the fine line that divides all opposites, we may discover that the edge is razor thin. We could quickly find ourselves falling over to the other side, becoming authoritarian and arrogant—self-absorbed by our own imagined importance and believing in delusions of grandeur. This could generate an inflated ego that can easily be punctured.

Additionally, this card admonishes us to live our own lives and generate our own experiences rather than seeking vicarious fulfillment through others. Fear of active participation can make us withdraw into a safe shell where our only contact with the world is through sanitized or second-hand avenues such as television and books.

Keeping our balance as we navigate the edge will grant us both intellect and insight. Accessing past experience while not dwelling in it will help us remain grounded in the present and project a clear-cut path to our future.

ORION

Though desert sands may parch my throat,
sting my skin, and blind my sight,
still I march with calm resolve
through the darkness of the night.

For I know that deep beneath
this lifeless land a mighty river flows
to quench my thirst and bring relief
from the painful path I chose.

30th Millennium of the Black Empire
Diary entry 13:

The weather is cold and dreary, as I was warned, here on the "Desolate Rim," which is not so different from the rest of this barren Empire planet, Hoova. I've traveled for four days on foot, over frozen mud and gravel, without another sign of life except for an occasional Black Empire enforcer craft surveying the horizon. Luckily, they don't bother to scan the interior of this section since it is beyond their psychic shield.

I thought there would be more of us out here. I know scores of resisters within the Designated Zone who have been taught "the methods" by the Underground League. I can't be the only one who's made it through . . . something must be wrong. According to the League's evacuation roster, groups of forty would make their way to the rendezvous spot on Hoova over the course of several days. The departure of refugees would be staggered so as to not attract suspicion. Cargo ships from the Aquar system have free passage into Orion territory. After decades of commerce here, they are all too aware of the deplorable actions of the Emperor's regime and have agreed to provide safe passage for us to the peaceful planets in the Sirius system.

Rumor has it that if a person dies outside the Empire's psychic net, then that soul is not automatically ensnared in the Emperor's astral trap of enforced reincarnation. I rejoice to think that my spirit might one day be free rather than being continually born into slavery within the Empire millennium after millennium. I hope it's true.

Hopefully the other workers like myself will all find "the methods" in their own time. So far it is the only way through the psychic barrier—and any possibility for freedom.

I keep one page from the Book of Methods in a pouch that hangs around my neck, lying close to my heart. I no longer have to remove it to read the words—they are impressed in my mind like the first sweet kiss from Simona's lips, may she rest in peace. It reads:

> For millennia we have fought for freedom against the evil Empire. We have lost our families, our property, and our dignity, but in the darkest times a miracle appeared. Out of Devon came a man with the wisdom of a thousand men. He gave us tools to regain our inner strength and hope. They are "the methods":

> The road to freedom is forged with the mind, not through battle. We will never create sovereignty through the hatred of oppression, but only through the love of freedom itself.

> > To eliminate war, love peace.
> > To eliminate injustice, love justice.
> > To eliminate poverty, love abundance.
> > To eliminate illness, love health.
> > Love and forgive those who persecute you, for

hatred will only bind you to them.
Become free within and the world around you
will allow you freedom.

As I sit warming my feet over a small fire, I look back to the horizon toward the Empire. There is a glow in my heart, and I know I am finally free.

The sharpest point of the Orion message is quite obvious. When we are confronted with obstacles, we should not resist them. Strength is gained by accepting blocks as opportunities. If we look for the lesson within and let go, we are released from oppressive ideas.

Orion energy deals with issues of fear, control, and domination, as well as situations dealing with bureaucracy and power structures. If the card of Orion has marched into our lives today, it is commanding that we take responsibility for our own knowledge and spiritual freedom rather than waiting to be rescued.

It may be warning us to not fall into the shadow side of this card, such as the dogma of ritualized institutions of learning or religion. We may need to separate ourselves from mass beliefs in order to find our own unique individualism. We must not succumb to the status quo or follow blindly.

One aspect of the Orion card is the strength to ignore intimidation by organizations—private, political, or theological—no matter how convincing their illusions of domination may be. The vibration of every individual determines how impervious he or she is to the negative effects of establishment.

PLEIADES

Suckling the full breast of life
for rich chocolate liqueurs of love,
I drink.
Rolling them round and round
in my receptive mouth of gratitude,
I savor.
Tasting the nectar sweetening
each breath of eternal beauty,
I breathe.
As deep belly gulps of abundance
satisfy my soul,
I sigh
and lick my lips!

Welcome! Have you just recently died and found yourself a graduate of the Earthly reincarnational cycle with a grade of eighty or above? If so, come with us. You are a candidate for consideration into the Tau Ceti system. Please adjust your consciousness to fourth density—250,000 cycles per second—and enter gate five. However, if you achieved a grade of ninety or above, you have earned the opportunity for bliss in the Pleiadian paradigm. Please align your vibrational frequency to high fourth density—333,000 cycles per second—and proceed to gate seven. Thank you.

You lucky sentient! As an Earth alumni with a score of ninety or above, you now hold membership in a very exclusive fraternity: the "PPP," or the "Preparing for Pleiadian Pleasures," club. This is a short preview of what you can expect in the Pleiadian paradise. Mind you, the population is kept at an uncrowded thirty-three million, so the line is quite long, but the wait is definitely worth it. For now, relax your astral bodies and open your auras . . . next stop, the Pleiades.

Welcome to the planet Erra! The first leg of your tour is the physical-body–fitting salon where you can select either the male or the female humanoid structure of your choice. As you can see, all physiques are perfectly proportioned, naturally muscular with extraordinary flexibility, and resistant to all disease. They are guaranteed for one thousand years or until ascension into the Infinite, whichever comes first, according to your desire.

Pleiadian corporeal forms are considered the most beautiful in the galaxy; they are designed to experience the height of sensuality and built to accommodate the erotic appetite their evocative chemistry arouses. As you may have guessed by now, passion is the national pastime in the Pleiades.

Leave your Visa card at home because you don't need money in the Pleiades. There is always enough of everything for everyone, naturally and synchronistically. With unlimited varieties of fruits and vegetables growing wild, food is abundant if you desire to partake, although consumption is purely for enjoyment—Pleiadians are automatically sustained by the breath of life. Housing is freely available but optional, as Pleiadians spend most of their time outdoors and traveling to neighboring worlds. All of the inhabited planets in the Pleiades have wonderfully temperate climates, and sleeping under the stars is most common.

All fuel required for "toys" is gratuitous. The Pleiadians have harnessed the electromagnetic field of the planet—an unlimited source of natural, nonpolluting energy.

If polarity is your thing, don't stop here! The Pleiadian emotional spectrum is limited to constant unconditional love, compassion, and ecstasy. If you have had enough slumming around the murky swamp of Earth emotionality, you'll find this psychic atmosphere of infinite light a refreshing and invigorating change of pace. Openness and positive thinking are the orders of the day in this telepathic retreat . . .

This is the end of your tour. If you exit here, it will be the beginning of many lifetimes of harmony and fun. We invite you to unbridle your creative self-expression and bask in the boundless personal freedom of this romantic getaway. And remember us, Incarnation Concepts, next time you're looking for the adventure of many lifetimes.

If Pleiadian flames are licking at our feet today, we'd better watch where we step . . . secret liaisons and spontaneous romantic interludes of absolute abandon are flirting with our future. It is also possible that lifetime loves may be lurking around the next corner.

But to fully enter the Pleiadian paradigm requires that we erase the earthly concept of scarcity and dissolve all traces of undeservability. We can get off to a good start by pampering ourselves with glorious episodes of self-indulgence.

Uninhibited displays of compassion are specialties on the Pleiadian menu for a full life, topped by complete self-acceptance and absolute freedom to be who we are at every moment. So the bell is ringing for a Pleiadian break from the earthly constraints of limitation and struggle. Vacations, massages, and candlelight dinners are beckoning.

It is true that Pleiadians know how to party, but we

must beware of what lurks in the shadows. To "trip the light fantastic" does not translate to an intoxicated free-for-all. Pleiadians maintain their magnificent physiques and sharp psychic senses with healthy moderation. To them, gormandizing and gluttony are only rumors about the goings on of much denser realities.

It may appear that Pleiadians are foot loose and fancy free, but they approach their unconstrained lifestyle respectfully. True freedom is not taken for granted, nor is it expressed in frivolous ways.

REPTILIAN

Slithering,
slimy,
scaly thing.
Your fangs rip,
your claws sting.
You're wild and unpredictable
and should return to swampy places,
until you've learned respect
for all other races!

University of Genetic Engineering
History 1117
Subject: Anomalous Mutations in the Milky Way Galaxy
Transcript: Star date 42115-31
Class: Lizard/Reptilian

Attention class! Come to order, please. Today's lesson is one that I, as a genetic historian, find most fascinating. The variety of lizard/reptilian creatures—and the diverse avenues of evolution they have followed—is a subject that demands many hours of research to appreciate. Since all of you are studying to become engineers and not historians, the university requires I give you only a basic understanding of the subject. So it is my hope that someday you will take it upon yourselves to delve deeper into this engrossing subject.

Because of the limitations of this class, we will focus on twentieth-century Earth, or Terra, where many split-offs of this reptilian species flourished at one time. Pulling from several recovered documents, the following were the standard definitions of the time:

Reptile: air-breathing vertebrate from the class reptilia. Characteristics include a three-chambered heart and a bony skeleton covered by dry scales or horny plates. Common reptiles are snakes, lizards, turtles, and crocodilians.

Lizard: any scaly reptile having a long body, four legs, and a long tail, as in the chameleon, iguana, or gecko families.

What is most intriguing about the findings of Earth history in regard to this matter is not what was written, but what was obviously left out of their authorized recordings. There were numerous disturbing, unofficial accounts of reptiles that progressed into sentient, two-legged beings.

It is most likely they developed off planet, but it is conceivable that their genetic codes were derived from Earth reptilian DNA in the earliest stages of Earth's evolution. Of course, this is purely speculation, but the material we have gathered about the physical characteristics of these Reptilians—that they had webbed appendages, fanged teeth, claws, and scaly covering—suggests there must be a connection. Curiously enough, they apparently developed superior mental abilities, providing them with such intellectual achievements as space travel—a vast departure from the native Earth species.

The few but poignant descriptions found in Earth archaeology describing these mutations of evolution are extremely similar to reports of reptilian types that frequented planets on the other side of the Milky Way Galaxy. These cumulative stories validate our suspicions that these mentally advanced entities were common but clandestine in their interactions with the planets they visited.

Their agenda was similar to the infamous silent invasion of the Grey aliens on planet Earth in the same historical time period. But as disturbing as the accounts of the Grey aliens' enforced genetic program were, there was a more sympathetic relationship between the Terrans and the Greys than with the Reptilians.

The Reptilians, also locally known as the Lizzies, were not simply undeveloped emotionally; they were cold-blooded primitives curious about genetic manipulation and unfortunately intellectually capable of satisfying their meddlesome nature by dominating more vulnerable species.

Their tactics were hostile—damaging to others both psychologically and physically, and earning them the reputation of the most malevolent of all extraterrestrial visitors.

It is logical that these scoundrels were responsible for the colloquial name-calling of "reptile" and "lizard" being most vehement insults. Such names were synonymous with the qualities despicable, contemptible, mean, treacherous, and harmful.

I think that just about covers the basics. Any questions?

When the Reptilian raises its ugly head, we'd better beware! It's time for us to get on another track; a 180-degree turn would be appropriate, and no later than immediately would be wise. The very least we can glean from this card is to proceed with caution and to realize that there are going to be some bumps in the road ahead if we are committed to the direction we are going. Consideration of an alternate path could provide a smoother ride.

It's most likely that the Reptilian is telling us that we are responding from an unconscious, primal mode of survival. Perhaps we are unknowingly looking to feed the monster of domination and control, so we need to examine our motivations with vigilance.

We must pinpoint the exact energy that is moving us in order to obtain clarity. Considering the ramifications of our actions is also crucial: How will our deeds affect the situation and all of those involved?

This card reflects the shadow side of our soul.

When we are face-to-face with the Reptilian, we can be assured that our most ancient and archetypal fears will rise to the surface and demand our attention, if not completely run away with us.

The positive aspect of this card is the foretelling of opportunity awaiting us to dive head first into our deepest unconscious dreads and challenge them to a good fight. Once we muster our courage and look at our fears directly, we soon discover that they are often little more than paper dragons.

Meditation and introspection are the nets to ensnare our excitable savage nature and domesticate it into a loving companion. Shedding light on the animal within is the sure way to tame the beast and brighten the future.

SIRIUS

I've never seen a trouble
that didn't burst like a bubble
on the tip of my sharp wit.
I've never had a pain
that didn't melt in the rain
when I've kept my spirit lit.
A foggy day will brighten
when I seek to lighten
the way I view all things.
I make sure that I play
a little every day
and enjoy the gifts life brings.

Starwatcher the dolphin burst from the ocean's surface in a splash of salt spray. The russet light of the setting sun glinted from his shiny wet skin as he joyfully somersaulted through the air and landed back in the water with a happy slap of his tail.

He loved this twilight hour, not only because the horizon was aglow with incandescent color, but because dusk preceded the night, when Starwatcher could live up to his name. Every evening when the skies were clear, he would bob for hours upon the gentle waves, peering at the bright point of light the humans called Sirius. It was a beautiful star, brilliant and blue-white—the brightest star in the sky. But that is not what held his fascination. Starwatcher had a friend way up there to whom he could talk with his mind.

Starwatcher understood that his telepathic friend was neither dolphin nor human, but that didn't matter. Whatever he was, he radiated the most intensely ecstatic energy Starwatcher had ever felt, so the dolphin eagerly awaited these nocturnal communications.

The Sirius entity told Starwatcher that his people had once been in contact with humans as well as with dolphins, but that was a long time past, during the reign of Atlantis. Back then, humans were as telepathic as dolphins and the two species were fast friends. But after the humans destroyed their island paradise through their own folly, they lost the ability to hear the dolphins' thoughts. Humans' minds had become filled with fear, so there was room for little else.

Whenever Starwatcher remembered the stories of ancient Atlantis, he was saddened. He yearned for the camaraderie of his human brothers and sisters, but only on rare occasions did one of their kind venture into the water to seek the dolphins out.

However, Starwatcher's Sirius friend assured him that the time was fast approaching when the humans would remember their kin in the sea and their ancient mentors among the stars. Starwatcher anticipated that future with great longing and dearly hoped he would live to see the day when dolphins and humans would once again play together as freely as he swam through the sparkling sea.

The Sirius card is not serious at all; it is absolutely the contrary. Sirius energy swells with joy. It absorbs every last drop of pleasure and peace, then sends it back out in a rippling wave of gratitude. This brilliant, effervescent intelligence floods our minds with illumination and fills our lives with harmony.

When Sirius rises to the surface, it is a tugging from our inner child to remember the innocence of yesteryear. We are called to immerse ourselves in the natural trust, freedom, and faith of the inexperienced—to bask in the unblemished simplicity of those still wet behind the ears.

But once we have tested the placid waters of renewal, we must not get caught up in the current of unaccountability and stagnate in a blasé sea of indifference. The tide of lightheartedness can easily turn to absentmindedness if left unchanneled.

Properly recognized, Sirius energy pronounces the potential for great creativity and re-creation. This is a time to release ourselves from the preconceived notions of our past and to look toward a shining future full of promise and delightful surprises.

Bathing in the Sirius energy opens us to many levels of information that we can integrate within ourselves, propelling us to new heights of artistic, emotional, mental, and spiritual expression. This card inspires us and keeps us buoyant so that we may stay on the crest of success.

ZETA

You come for me
from between realities.
You take from me
to feed the secret soul of destiny.
I look into your eyes
and see eternity.
You are calling.
But I refuse to answer for all of mankind
For I am only one,
yet I'm also one
of . . . you.

Internet Communication:

Call me the "Man in Black." I cannot reveal my true identity because the following information is classified "Above Top Secret," and revealing it could get me killed— or worse. And, believe me, there is something worse.

I have become an unwitting participant in an unconscionable conspiracy. I have been shown secret documents and evidence that proves beyond the shadow of a doubt that our government is in cooperation with an extraterrestrial intelligence in an ongoing program of human abduction.

These are the same aliens that have been reported by thousands of people since the 1947 UFO crash near Roswell, New Mexico, and that are infamously known as the "Greys." They originate from a star system in the constellation of Zeta Reticulum, which is approximately thirty-eight light-years from Earth. These small-framed, humanoid creatures range in size from three and one-half to five feet tall and exhibit large, bald heads and oversized, pitch-black eyes. Their species possesses a hive mentality, similar to that of an ant colony: Each one is a part of, and controlled by, one consciousness. They not only lack individualism but also seem devoid of emotion or compassion. However, these unsocial characteristics have not detoured them from evolving a vast intellect and superior technology.

These aliens are secretly carrying out genetic experiments on humans for the purpose of creating a new hybrid race that is a cross between both our species. People are abducted from their homes, most often while they are asleep. Drugs and psychic manipulation are used on these abductees to suppress the memories of the encounters so that when recollections surface they are often mistaken for dreams.

Why the aliens need to do this, and with such clandestine methods, is as much a mystery to the secret government as it is to those they abduct. But one conjecture is that they are preserving our DNA in the event of a self-inflicted ecological collapse. There are intriguing suspicions that the aliens may be coming to us from our own future.

Unfortunately, this is the extent of the information I can risk divulging at this time, but I assure you that there is more to come. It is my personal belief, and the belief of a select few within the secret government, that it would be more beneficial for humanity to be exposed to this information than to keep "protecting" them from the truth. We are depending on you to assist us in exposing this iniquitous cover-up.

The Zeta card insists that we take a closer look at our relationships and circumstances to see where there may be a lack of communication or emotional connection. With most issues there is more than that which is immediately apparent on the surface. There may be secrets that need to be revealed or hidden agendas that should be exposed. We may even be keeping secrets from ourselves or be involved in situations that all aspects of our consciousness may not be in agreement with. Honesty with everyone in our lives is mandatory, but it is even more essential that we be candidly introspective.

Zeta demands that we look beyond who we believe ourselves to be and seek to be more aware of our totality. We must awaken within the dream and discover the portions of our being that have long remained concealed.

This card suggests we may have become unbalanced by developing and depending on our left brain too much. Our processes may be too logical, too intellectual, while our emotions are being ignored or suppressed; more compassion and less detachment are called for. Seeking the support of the right-brain, intuitive self will bring balance.

Additionally, attracting Zeta may mean we need to examine our personal boundaries, beliefs, and definitions and clarify who we are so as not to be "invaded" by realities that are not of our preference. Simultaneously, this card hints that we may have our own hidden agendas and agreements to play a part in a "bigger picture" even if we are consciously out of touch with that higher purpose.

Regardless of how overpowering a dilemma may seem, the Zeta card refreshes our knowing that there is always help available from "inside information" to assist us in remedying any situation. When we openly receive the information we get from within, whether it comes from spirit guides, God/Goddess, or our own instincts, the reward is more and more guidance. If we do not acknowledge the inner communications because they may seem illogical, we cut ourselves off from our source.

As all symbols are multilayered, this card also warns us to expect the unexpected and by all means to question authority. But the most critical warning echoed from the Zeta aspect of our future selves is to wait no longer to get personally involved in healing Mother Earth. Zeta warns: If there are ideas we have been considering implementing or actions we could take to assist the planet, now is the time!

SHIPS

CARD	ATTRIBUTE
Probe	Observer
Pod	Personal Journey
Scout	Teamwork/ Marriage
Explorer	Curiosity
Research	Knowledge
Medical	Healing
Cargo	Abundance
Tour	Leisure
Battleship	Conflict
Mothership	Home/Mother
The Fleet	Sweeping Change
Space Station	Source

SHIPS

Certainly the most well-recognized symbol of the entire extraterrestrial phenomenon, UFOs of one kind or another have been reported by multitudes of people throughout recorded history. Some of the designs in this system are based on photographic evidence or eye-witness accounts, while a few ships are extrapolations based on the energy concepts they represent.

The energy dynamic of the ships is connected to movement, journeys, and processes within our consciousness.

SHIPS

PROBE

PROBE

Another assignment . . . finally! I was beginning to think they had forgotten about me down here. I can't wait to leave this hanger and dust myself off. Here comes my program: investigate planet surface . . . feed data to main computer . . . return at designated time code 8.173.

The gate is opening. I'm out of here! Wow, does this feel great! Vega reporting to Mother: Descending through thick cumulus cloud covering. The H_2O molecules are so dense in here I can't see an inch in front of my lenses . . . I'm going to have to use my feeling sensors to navigate. Its been a long time since I've surfed through clouds.

The atmosphere is clearing. I'm scanning the surface now, detecting electromagnetic signatures of carbon-based life everywhere. I'm going in to take a closer look. There are indications of so many species it might take years to analyze this place: land masses covered with vegetation, insects, and animals . . . large bodies of water brimming with creatures of all shapes and sizes. . . . Incredible! I've never recorded anything like this!

SPLASH! I'm under the water now. It's a pleasing 70 degrees. A lifeform with long tentacles is approaching.

I wonder if this may be my first contact with a sentient being. Directly to my left are thousands of small, colorful creatures moving in unison. They must like each other a lot the way they stick so close together.

Mother, I don't think we're alone in checking out this planet—it looks like a giant research ship straight ahead. Wait . . . it's sending some kind of communication! Music— it's singing! This is no ship; it's alive! This is the most fascinating place I've ever scanned.

Mother, we need to discuss this. I've barely glimpsed a small segment of this planet and my time is almost up, but I couldn't bear to leave now. Why don't you pick me up sometime next century and I'll have a complete rundown for you. Over and out!

P.S. Don't hurry!

The Probe is our signal to investigate what's happening around us or within a particular situation that demands our attention. No detail is too small or insignificant, and in order to project a complete picture, we need to compile as much data as possible. By following this program, we may also be guided to discover new attributes we might have overlooked before that could enrich our overall comprehension of how we view life.

The most important property of the Probe energy is the ability to remain an objective observer. Collecting data is the Probe's expertise. This particular talent—not to be clouded by too many opinions, expectations, or judgments—is the quality from which we can most benefit at this juncture.

If we are to truly appreciate the power of the Probe appearing in our world today, we will need to understand the appropriateness of remaining emotionally uninvolved in whatever circumstances are present until all aspects of the condition are fully analyzed and understood. This is one of those delicate times that calls for loving detachment. We must take our time and pay attention because it's often easy to be carried away by our desire to get where we think we're going and to forget to take time to smell the roses.

POD

Amber sat cross-legged in the very center of the pod's tiny cabin. She was deep in her meditation as the little ship carried her silently through the solitude of space, the distant stars softly reflecting in its burnished pewter skin.

The small pod knew, in its automated memory, where Amber was going so there was no need for her to monitor the controls. However, it was limited in its propulsion power; this was going to be long trip.

Amber could just as easily have booked passage on one of the new lightcruisers that offered every conceivable amenity and would have delivered her to her destination in a fraction of the time. She chose the spartan pod ship instead because she knew that the one person she needed to spend time with was herself.

Her life was happy and fulfilling, but recently she found it harder and harder to find time to be alone. Though Amber's civilization was very advanced and wanted for nothing, it was easy to become caught up in the furious pace and ecstatic drive of twenty billion expressive souls. Before you knew it, you were one among many, instead of one out of many.

Amber's awareness continued to drift inward until she felt complete tranquillity. She was actually surprised at the ease and speed at which she reached her peaceful center. The becalming serenity washed away all of her concerns until her mind was as empty as the womb of endless black space that surrounded the pod. A warm, loving vibration flooded her body and soul; she was once again one with the universe, floating in the love of the Infinite.

Slowly, Amber opened her eyes and viewed the pod's intimate interior with appreciation for the revelation the small spacecraft had afforded her. She realized she could rely on this experience to be there for her in the future when she found herself lost in the hustle of everyday life.

Now she was ready for her journey's end, where she could meet and interact with others. Once again Amber knew who she was: a unique, cherished, and unconditionally supported aspect of All That Is.

If we have drawn the Pod card, we are being taken on a personal journey of introspection and self-awareness.

It may be long past due for us to turn our sights inward and engage in quiet reflection. Though we often search for fulfillment through the objects, places, and people in the outside world, it is a time-honored truth that all our personal answers are within us.

Such a journey may require that we seek solitude so that the silence, as in the vastness of space, can help us to hear the faint whisper of wisdom that resides in the center of our beingness. The Pod, our private little bubble, gently turns our attention toward issues of intimacy and sharpens our listening skills, both inward and outward. This is essential, for if we do not know who we are, then our true selves will be absent from all relationships.

It may require a great deal of courage to begin such an exploration of self-discovery, for we have hidden many fears within the dark crevasses of our unconsciousness. We are full of twisting paths and shadowy reflections; we can fall into the downward spiral of self-uncertainty and become lost in a gloomy depression that admits no light and no relief.

It is critical that we remember that fear is just a messenger that solicits our attention to information about ourselves that requires processing and integration. When we cease to think of ourselves as a collection of conflicting parts and instead view ourselves holistically, we can begin to discover who we really are.

Sometimes the easiest way to begin to realize our true identity is to admit that we don't actually know ourselves. We can then give ourselves permission to drop our limiting definitions and allow the Infinite to reveal who it is we were created to be.

SHIPS

SCOUT

SC⚲UT

The small scout craft flew low and slow over the rocky terrain. Sitting at their consoles in the ship's tiny cabin, Brin and Kiri worked the controls as though they were a single being. They often thought of themselves that way—as one mind sharing two bodies. They had trained together and been copilots in this ship for years. Brin and Kiri knew each other's preferences; they knew each other's thoughts. They had become more than colleagues . . . they were family . . . they were one.

This synergistic rapport was common with scout craft teams, for they were always the first ships in unexplored space and pointed the way for the larger explorer and research ships to follow. Brin and Kiri's talents complemented each other's well, with Brin's skills filling the gap in Kiri's experience and Kiri doing the same for Brin.

They had spied this planet on their sensors while reconnoitering a new star system, and the initial scans seemed most promising. The planet was inhabited, however, so Kiri suggested, with the slightest of glances, that they survey a remote area at night. Brin understood the look, just as he knew all of her gestures by heart.

They guided their little craft between the desert outcrops with eyes glued to the viewscreen. Kiri caught the sudden tensing in Brin's posture and stopped the ship immediately.

There before them was a group of beings sitting around a fire. The beings stood up and stared at the scout craft, eyes wide with fright.

Brin quickly hit the control, and the ship leapt skyward

at breathtaking speed, leaving the people below in open-mouthed shock. Once in orbit high above the blue planet, Kiri and Brin looked at each other and laughed. They knew in an instant that both they and the surprised dwellers down below would have new stories to share back home.

The Scout card is the mark of marriage, whether in love or business, and represents the shared give-and-take that accompanies teamwork and all harmonious interactions. Symbolizing the special bond that is forged within intimate relationships, be they with our closest friends and family members or the fires of passion that engulf soul mates, Scout embraces interconnectedness.

When two or more people come together in this energy, then synergy, telepathy, and synchronicity abound. But our most valuable ties are not necessarily limited to physical counterparts. Besides the kinship we feel with our animal brothers and sisters and the planet, the connection we have to the nonphysical realms of our higher selves, our ancestor spirits, and our spirit guides are perhaps the most dear of all. Nor can we forget the significance of our relationship to our life's work.

This card is a recognition of all the supportive and trea-sured links we have made in this lifetime. It encourages us to give glorious thanks and acknowledgment to the contri-bution these relationships have made to the quality of our existence.

Of course, if celebration of our relationships has not crossed our minds lately, perhaps this card is suggesting it is time to scout around and discover what might be inter-fering with our ability to fully give and receive in the con-text of close unions.

The reverse of Scout's energy is often expressed as the

phrase "Familiarity breeds contempt." It reveals that when we are not happy with ourselves, we tend to project our insecurities or suppressed anger on those closest to us.

Relationships are for the purpose of allowing us to learn more about ourselves by observing the attributes reflected in our partners. If we are in denial concerning our fears, we can straitjacket the union by trying to turn it into what we think we need for protection, rather than allowing the relationship to be what it really is and serve us in a natural way.

If we recognize that we are forcing the relationship to move in accord with our expectations, then we can relax our grip and enjoy the experience of the friendship and intimacy. It might also become apparent that in certain situations that are not serving us, the most loving thing we could choose, for others and ourselves, would be to let the relationship go. It will then be possible to either change in ways that will allow it to continue or make room for a more appropriate and beneficial relationship to appear. Love is not stagnant. It can be felt only through the process of exchange. We cannot reciprocate freely until we are willing to greet love with an open heart.

SHIPS

EXPLORER

EXPLORER SHIP

"**W**e have been so many places in the galaxy," said Explorer One.

"We have discovered so many new things," said Explorer Two.

Explorer Three knew they were both right. The trio had begun their mission a long time ago, hopping from world to world in their spectacular ship. And it *is* spectacular, mused Explorer Three.

The sophisticated craft bristled with dozens of sensors, antennae, and analyzing apparatuses. The crew could scan and record from the highest-dimensional energies to the smallest speck of matter. No secrets were hidden from them for too long.

It also took a special kind of being to be an explorer, the three knew: a being with a childlike curiosity, a sense of adventure, and, above all, persistence.

"I see something interesting on the scanner," chimed One.

Two and Three were immediately attentive. They had discovered so many things, it was easy to take a new find for granted. But if Explorer One thought what he was seeing was "interesting," that meant it might be something worthy of a few minutes of their time.

They set a course for the small remote asteroid that had alerted their sensors and flew their ship right into an enormous, deep cave in the center of a large crater. Explorer Two activated the ship's floodlights, but the beams fell into the darkness, revealing nothing.

Finally, their sensors emitted a squeal of discovery! There, hovering in the air before them, was a smooth, featureless sphere. It gleamed in their searchlights like a radiant pearl.

Explorer One squinted into his scanner, waiting for the sensors to analyze what they had found. Tense moments passed as all three explorers waited for the sphere to give up its secrets.

Finally, Explorer One turned from the scanner and faced his companions, barely able to contain his excitement. Mischief glinted in his eyes as he savored their excruciating anticipation.

"We couldn't have hoped for anything better," he teased.

"What is it? What is it?" Two and Three pleaded in unison.

Explorer One took a breath. Slowly, deliberately, and with great glee, he said, "I don't know!"

If our insatiable curiosity has invited a visit from the Explorer Ship, then we are open to exploring the unknown mysteries of creation. This is the card of the sorcerer, the scientist, the artist, and the shaman—that portion of our awareness that seeks to know all that can be known and then explores further beyond those boundaries.

With this card, we are in the abyss, in uncharted waters with nothing to guide us but imagination and intuition. We are out on a limb, humbly asking the Infinite to share the secrets of its incomprehensible existence.

The Explorer Ship invites us to go where no one has gone before, and we must be prepared to expect the unexpected. While in this energy, we are sustained by the thrill of the search, seduced by the lure of the labyrinth, and strengthened by the revelations of each sub-rosa skeleton brought to light.

To channel this card, we must be willing to let change be the only constant in our lives and learn to derive succor from uncertainty. If we can master this polymorphic reality, then we will be capable of opening an inexhaustible array of conduits to new, unknown realms of wonder and magic.

Exploring the unexplored also requires great respect and validation for all the ways creation can express itself. If we carry our primal fears and arrogant assumptions with us into pristine territory, we may cloak its denizens in our own demonic design rather than perceive these "foreigners" in their own light of truth.

SHIPS

RESEARCH

RESEARCH SHIP

"It's always something," the professor chuckled to himself. He was pretty thin, even for a being of his species, because he never stopped running.

Up and down, back and forth, from bridge to science station, the wizened tutor was never in one part of the ship for too long. New data coming in from that star, an unclassified plant from that world, an unusual weather pattern forming in a gas-giant planet—there was just so much to learn!

"And I'm suppose to have time to teach!" he muttered as he scurried over to a bank of information analyzers. "I can barely keep up with the discoveries sent back by the explorer ships, and yet they want me to train the apprentice data compilers as well."

The elder academician glanced at the ship's chronometer and clapped his hands in delight. He hurried from the lab with a hasty nod to his fellow professors and locked himself in the one room aboard the research ship where he could find a moment's solace: the library.

Banks and banks of gleaming, crystalline holocubes, each of which stored more than ten trillion bits of information, lined the walls near the viewing booths. The professor nestled into a soundproof chamber and popped his favorite cube into the image projection slot.

He was immediately surrounded by a seemingly solid and realistic countryside setting. Tall trees rustled in the breeze, the sound of their leaves mingling with the rhythmic crashing of the waves from an inviting beach.

The professor loved these peaceful moments, and in spite of the crusty exterior he presented to his colleagues and students, he truly loved his work as well. The universe was such a marvel of organized information that one could spend a million lifetimes learning the smallest fraction of it.

Unexpectedly, a small figure began to walk up the beach in the professor's holographic projection. All at once, it turned and headed right for him.

"Computer! There were no people in this recording before!" the professor protested.

"Hi, professor," the young man called.

"Apprentice! What are you doing here?" retorted the professor.

"Oh, I found a way to write myself into the program. It's time for class and the other students bet me I couldn't find a way in. Looks like they lost."

The professor laughed: the old pedagogue had taught somebody something after all. He shook his head and left the library, running down the ship's corridor. "It's always something," he clucked to himself as he slid into the lab, the faces of his friends and apprentices smiling in anticipation of their mentor's wisdom.

The Research Ship is the card that deals with education and the application of knowledge. When we have spent time gathering and analyzing information, we look for avenues through which to express our newly found insights and to pass our discoveries on to others to adapt for multitudinous uses. This card instructs us in the importance of sharing and distributing what our lessons have taught us, in ways that best serve the good of all.

It is also time for us to search out new knowledge, lest we fall into repetition and intellectual stagnation.

Imagination is a guiding principle of this energy, along with the initiative to combine necessity and experience for producing new, inventive solutions to the enticing puzzles in our lives.

The curriculum of this card also contains the possibility of intellectual snobbery. This can seal us in our ivory towers as we judgmentally label others as our inferiors.

Turned negatively upon itself, this energy can convert us into social recluses, hidden away from public view and lost in our own dry world of facts and figures with no practical application. Instead of gaining new knowledge and insights, we can fixate on outdated information and archaic notions that rapidly crumble in the light of new discoveries and evolving theories.

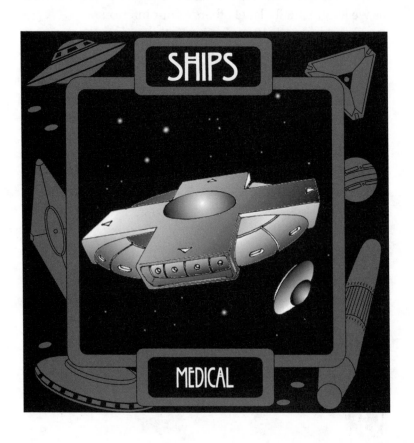

SHIPS

MEDICAL

MEDICAL SHIP

Oanna imagined the pressure of the medical ship's trans-light speed crushing her into the padded pilot's seat, though she knew that the craft's internal gravity would never allow that to happen. Her heart sounded like a drum in her ears, and the flashing red emergency light reminded her of the blood pumping through her temples.

She had experienced an adrenalin rush in countless life and death situations before, but this was different. This time, it was her own daughter, Maya, who had sent the distress signal, and Oanna could not help but fear the worst.

Maya was in charge of a scouting expedition to an uncharted sector of the galaxy. It was her first command mission, and Oanna was very proud of her daughter. She had also worried a bit, since they never knew what might happen in unexplored space. Yet she knew it was part of the job, and she certainly wouldn't come between Maya and her career.

But now it seemed that all her worries might come true. There had been no other signal after the initial emergency beacon. Oanna had no way of knowing whether her daughter was merely injured or . . . NO! She couldn't think about that. She focused on the control panel, trying to squeeze every drop of speed she could from her ship's straining engines.

Every passing moment was a frozen forever as Oanna pushed the sensors to the limit, scanning for Maya's disabled ship. The space ahead was strewn with rocky asteroids, which made her task all the more difficult.

Oanna squinted at the readout as if her will alone might

reach out and grab Maya's craft. Then she saw it. One of the small specks on her scanner was just a bit too reflective for an asteroid—even for a chunk of ice. She had found them!

She locked the computer on automatic and scrambled for her emergency kit. In seconds, the medical ship docked with the badly damaged scout craft, and Oanna dove through the connecting airlock.

The scout's interior was dark and silent. Oanna took a quick breath and readied herself. She pulled a lightglobe from her kit and switched it on, flooding the scout's cabin with soft yellow light. Her heart sank.

There on the floor lay her daughter and two crewmen; a small trickle of blood striped across Maya's forehead. Oanna took a quick scan with her instruments and thanked the Goddess in an exhale of relief . . . they were still alive.

She knelt over her daughter, and Maya's eyes flickered open as though from a deep dream. "I knew you would come," she murmured, then lapsed back into blackness.

Later, when they had all returned to the medical base and the patients were safely recovering, Oanna paid her daughter a visit. She knew that Maya loved the special sweets found on a single planet a hundred light-years away, and Oanna had made sure to bring the biggest box of them she could find.

Maya's laughter at the sight of the huge container told Oanna that her daughter was truly healing. "I was never worried," Maya assured her mother. "When I first lost consciousness, I could feel you holding me in your arms like you did when I was young. I knew, because of your love for me, that you would not give up until you found me."

"Yes," Oanna agreed, looking deeply into her daughter's sparkling eyes. "Love is where all healing begins."

Whether it is based on science or belief, healing is a self-generated state. Though miraculous cures can manifest in either paradigm, it takes a profound acceptance of ourselves and a deep willingness to process our personal issues in order to allow true healing to occur.

The Medical Ship, emergency lights flashing, also warns us to be keenly aware of our physical, mental, and emotional states. When we are discouraged or sick in our hearts, when we constantly expose ourselves to stressful situations, we inevitably wind up dis-eased.

This card prescribes that we clean up our diet, both literally and symbolically, taking in only those foods and ideologies that keep us energetic and light. Otherwise, we run the risk of contracting a metaphysical malaise that can quickly develop into a physical malignancy.

Drawing this card may also be a diagnosis that we are in denial about self-destructive, unconscious beliefs that keep us from lasting healing. We need to get in touch with these patterns, or we might orchestrate an accident to draw our attention to the unresolved emotional issues and force us to heal them through acceptance and integration.

Great faith is the sign of this card. It is always accompanied by the nurturing and supportive qualities that complete a true healer's "bedside manner."

If the Medical Ship has appeared in our chart today, we can greatly benefit by allowing our healing energies to flow, both to others and ourselves. All forms of medicine are sacred callings—invitations to be immersed in the healing waters of love.

CARGO SHIP

Excerpt from the captain's personal log:

My people used to sail the seas to taste the riches of the diverse cultures of our world. They were renowned for gathering and dispersing precious collectibles to anxiously awaiting ports.

Then we learned to fly in great metal birds, and we made our vast planet seem small. Exchanging wares was still a profitable enterprise though once exotic goods soon became commonplace.

Today we are starfarers who first took halting, tentative steps, jumping in little tin spaceships from planet to planet within our star system and finally leaping into the silent void between the stars. My crew and I now glide through velvet space, surrounded by the glistening shell of this great cargo ship, carrying all manner of riches from the diverse cultures of many worlds. Once again, we are disseminating rare and exquisite finds:

- Wines and liquors, intoxicating spirits distilled from the luscious fruits of faraway worlds.

- Beauty elixirs that change skin and eyes to any hue in the spectrum.

- Glistening fabrics spun with rare metals mined from the cores of collapsed stars.

- Crystals that enhance a person's psychic proclivities.

- Ancient manuscripts and artifacts that speak the forsaken histories of lost civilizations.

- Stardust ores that hold miraculous cures.

- Tidings from outlying regions of the cosmos.

How far we have come; yet as we sail the seas of the Infinite, we are still so like our merchant ancestors of long ago. We are ever captivated by awaiting undiscovered shores and the secret treasures they harbor.

Cargo Ship is the card of contacts and big business, of exchange and sweeping change. It calls upon us to be movers and shakers, givers and takers—to get down to business and to get our affairs in order. In drawing this energy, we are advised to pay attention to agreements and contracts, both on paper and verbal, making sure our intentions and desires are clearly spelled out.

This card symbolizes abundance and the diversity of riches, indicating that our ship may be about to come in. It may also represent rewards and recognition for a job well done.

However, portents of great wealth can throw some of us off balance. This is the time to be alerted to our own potential greed and the signs of avarice in those who operate from a fear of not having enough.

Great expansion accompanies this card, and we must be prepared for the level of responsibility on the flip side of the coin. Entrepreneurial endeavors can succeed beyond our wildest dreams if we remember that business is based on personal vision and unswerving belief in the services that we provide.

Above all, quality must reside in all aspects of any enterprise we undertake. While some may think the end justifies the means, we will soon realize that the means and the end are one and the same: what we sow is what we will reap.

TOUR SHIP

Sliding, gliding on waves of starlight, bathed in rainbow reflections of prismatic mists, the silver streamlined leisure craft rides the ethers on its grand tour. Each viewport frames an eager face waiting to behold the wonders of the universe: the majesty of the sweeping rings that crown a world of roiling hues; the beckoning, firefly lights of a million solar lanterns, sprinkled on a velvet field like tiny diamonds; the lone comet burning in the dark, its diaphanous tail flowing behind like the windblown tresses of some celestial spirit.

The tour guide, perched alone atop the ship in his crystal bubble, muses upon the vista that extends to infinity around him. Though he is a veteran of a thousand voyages, the vast universe still gifts him with mystery; he never flies the ship to the same sights twice.

Below decks in the plush cabins, stellar sojourners are pampered like monarchs by an attentive staff. A rich buffet of delicacies intoxicates their senses, and a parade of amusements captivates their curiosity. Their stories are as varied as the stars:

Here, an elder gentle being reclines in richly embroidered finery, having saved all of his days for this time of retirement and relaxation.

There, a lone traveler casts her fortune to the stars in search of a soul mate.

And yonder, a young couple on their honeymoon: their twin flames burn as brightly as Sirius as they dance, free from gravity's woes, to the symphony of the spheres.

For all who embark upon this passage to exotic ports of call, the tour guide is their eye in the night. He savors his calling with spiritual satisfaction. With each new sight that brings delight to a thousand curious eyes, their souls are gifted and their imaginations uplifted by the boundless treasures of creation.

The Tour Ship predicts calm seas and smooth sailing. This is a time to enjoy ourselves and partake of the sweet nectars of life; time to take a well-earned vacation—to relax and be refreshed.

This symbol points the way to the path of least resistance, where everything falls into place with the slightest touch and all our dreams come true. We can now laugh long and loud, without worry or doubt, for things will take care of themselves from here on out.

It is a time to be entertained, pampered, and catered to. We are encouraged to get away from the hectic world of schedules and deadlines—to live to the fullest and taste the rich treats of newly discovered paradises.

But the true danger in Eden was not the snake. Deep within our idyllic dream, we must remain alert, mindful that we do not drift into a lackluster stupor—the slack-jawed domain of the lethargic Lotus Eaters. Once we have succumbed to such languid torpor, we may become like the fly trapped in its amber prison or a lone explorer seeking to be saved from a deadly pit of quicksand.

We are entitled to enjoy the luxuries life has to offer. Sipping them slowly, like fine wine, will allow us to appreciate them over the course of the entire journey, instead of drowning our senses all at once and spending the sojourn in listless oblivion.

Finally, the Tour Ship may be sending a signal that we

are about to embark on an unexpected trip. This would be a good time for us to clean up any loose ends and have our business affairs and relationships in good shape so we can be free to enjoy the journey.

BATTLESHIP

The deck plates buckled beneath the gunners' boots, throwing the soldiers into the walls. The scorch of burning circuits filled their nostrils, and the battleship's corridors were soon choked with acrid smoke, making it difficult to see the enemy ships on the tactical screens.

"Damage report!" the officer screamed to the computer.

"Lateral control destroyed," the computer obediently toned. "Aft shields at 37 percent."

"Reserve power to aft shields," ordered the officer as he scrambled through the burning gangway, quickly assessing his troops' condition.

"Medic to station three," he called out, jumping into the laser-control cockpit occupied by an injured soldier.

"We can't hold against this many raiders, sir!" the soldier stammered, wiping the blood from his head wound and pretending to be all right.

"The medic's on his way. I'll take this station," the commander ordered, pounding at the flickering laser controls. "We've got to hold them just long enough for the colonists to reach the planetary defense net. Another three minutes is all we need!" He kicked the control panel in a frustrated rage, and the laser cannon flared back to life.

"You did it!" exclaimed the soldier.

A surge of inspiration struck the commander.

"Computer! Channel all ship's power to cannon three, and fire one five-second burst from the midship thruster."

The dazed soldier looked at his commanding officer with a blank stare. Had he gone mad? Lights began winking out all through the ship as power was routed to the cannon. The thruster fired, sending the wounded battleship into an awkward spin. The troops sat in the dark, sweating and choking; some were praying, for certainly they were all about to die.

Then the soldier understood. "The ship looks like it's dead," he announced.

"Let's hope the raiders think so, too," responded the commander with a smile.

The raiders, eager for a kill, took the bait and swarmed toward the crippled juggernaut to finish it off. As soon as they were all lined up in attack formation, the battleship commander tightened his grip on the firing control. The ship's rotation swept the cannon's lethal energy beam across the vacuum of space, catching the raiders completely by surprise. In moments their attack force was vaporized. The few smoldering metal shards that remained of their ships bounced harmlessly off the battleship's pockmarked hull.

The weary troops cheered as light and fresh air flooded the ship's gangways, clearing away the stench of battle. They all praised their commander's experience and quick-witted reaction.

"Today we won, and the colonists are safe," he reflected. "It is sad when conflicts cannot be settled by peaceful resolution. But in the face of those who would oppress us, we will always be on guard."

At first glance, the Battleship card would seem to encompass the energy of conflict, and it can certainly indicate a desperate situation in which all parties are at odds with each other. When our "buttons" are pushed or our sense of justice has been compromised, our tempers often flare in angry response to what we perceive as an attack upon ourselves or our cherished beliefs.

However, while it is sometimes true that remarks aimed in our direction may be caustic and "out of line," we should think twice before launching an equally vehement counter-attack. We may run the risk of escalating the situation into a full-scale war.

On the bright side, this card encourages us to stand up for our beliefs with clear resolve and to be watchful, around us and within ourselves, for those energies that might undermine our faith in what we know is true for us.

Yet being overly suspicious can decay into rampant paranoia, which, like any energy, will attract circumstances of similar vibration and perpetuate a self-fulfilling prophecy of doom.

Our outlook is best when authorized by both heart and mind. Then the Battleship can symbolize the upholding of honor, arriving at diplomatic resolutions, standing firmly in our truth in the face of oppression or opposition, and saving the day by knowing that a positive lesson or outcome can be pulled from the midst of the most challenging situations.

SHIPS

MOTHERSHIP

MOTHERSHIP

M other, you are always there
when I return in the dark of night.

O h, it is a welcome sight
to see your brilliant, guiding light.

T ell my family I have arrived
to share the tale of my trip,

H appy to be safe and warm,
deep within the mothership.

E arth is unlike any world
I have explored before.

R are animals and plants abound;
there are humans, and what's more,

S haring among them is truly rare,
for they are fearful to the core.

H ome is just a house to them—
four walls, a roof, a door.

I ponder their predicament
as we float here high above,

P erhaps they will never learn to respect
their mother's gift of love.

A mother's love is one of the most important factors in our ability to learn and grow into healthy, happy adults. It is now understood that if we are not given the opportunity to literally look into our mother's eyes immediately after birth, the necessary biological cues that we need in order to understand and process our new surroundings will not be passed on to us. Therefore, the Mothership card symbolizes the importance of complete support and unconditional love in all our actions, especially at the beginning of any new relationship.

Mother energy can nurture us in a way that allows us to find our own strength. However, if it is coming from a controlling attitude and fear of abandonment, it can become a smothering cloud that stunts our growth by passing that fear along to us.

This card, then, carries polarized meanings. Depending on the circumstances, it can represent the need to strengthen the bond of home and family, or it can suggest that it might be time to cut the apron strings and leave the nest in order to avoid negative codependence.

The Mothership card also may be announcing that we need to pay attention to matters that involve children, whether those already in our lives or those who have yet to be born. It reminds us that each action or project we support is another kind of offspring—the fruits of our labor.

As mother energy brings forth a new generation of ideas and awareness, it reminds us to take our family lineage—our heritage—into account as well. Building upon that progression in constructive ways will help us to leave the world a better place for all the children of Mother Earth.

THE FLEET

Scores of children and adults flock to the space station's viewports in anticipation of the arrival of the fleet. They excitedly press against the glass as the station lights dim, affording them a panoramic view of the starscape around them.

At first all is still and serene, the familiar constellations salting the black backdrop of infinity. Then a child points toward the distance and every eye follows. A long line of silvery saucers glides toward the station—the advance guards announcing the presence of the fleet!

Excitement mounts as the lead ships are followed by a group of larger craft: explorer ships, medical vessels, and swift battle cruisers of all sizes and configurations.

Laser beacons dance between the ships and the station's control tower as the first wave of the fleet is guided into the docking bays to disgorge the weary crews.

A gasp suddenly escapes from a newcomer in the crowd, and the gathering holds its collective breath. Row after row of titanic motherships stretch out of the blackness into the illuminating searchlights that arc around the station's perimeter.

Each cylinder is twenty miles in length. The iridescent cityships are resplendent with a fine lacework of running lights and glowing viewports.

The majestic leviathans spread out in a ring that surrounds the station, each gently docking with its appointed air lock like spokes on a cosmic wheel. The fleet is home to relax and regenerate, to share the stories of ten thousand adventures before voyaging forth once again into the vast expanse of the unknown.

To beacon The Fleet is to summon the angels. This is the energy of sweeping global change, of signs and omens and social transformation. When we soar at this altitude, we are in the company and under the guidance of compassionate energies that affect the lives of millions.

This is the card of initiation into higher realms of knowledge and power. This energy can manifest as healing light through enlightened individuals, such as Mahatma Gandhi, or, if polarized, as Plutonic darkness in tormented souls, such as Adolf Hitler. Within this symbol, we rally to acknowledge our ability to lead—to grab hold of a vision and follow it through—and to accept responsibility for the consequences of our actions.

If The Fleet has appeared on our horizon, we can be assured that it is time to gather all our thoughts and experiences and look for the interconnected patterns that point the way to our next goal or action. This card symbolizes the importance of deploying all our skills and bringing our combined resources to bear on the situation before us so that we can generate a self-perpetuating momentum that will see our task through to its conclusion.

However, if our communication, internal and external, is cut off or otherwise unclear, then our well-coordinated attempts will fall apart, each critical component scattering chaotically. This is a powerful energy when all factors are well thought out and people are allowed to use their true talents and strengths, but it quickly becomes unwieldy and cumbersome without the flagship of a strong, clear vision to orchestrate the essential elements.

SHIPS

SPACE STATION

SPACE STATION

I am the watcher. I float among the stars, guiding travelers to my safe haven. My beacons extend for light-years— electronic invitations to countless weary wanderers to come join their companions within the sphere of my hospitality.

I am a hive of activity. Tales of commerce and secret trysts, of battles and expanding civilizations, echo throughout my halls in the boisterous tongues and guarded whispers of a thousand starfaring cultures. Within me all ordinary needs can be met with extraordinary pleasure, as I provide the creature comforts to all of those who are hungry for the familiarities of home.

For the restless, my library is filled with magnificent odysseys. It is a custom in my inn that wayfarers leave record of their pilgrimages for the entertainment of those who will follow.

For the sore, in my parlors await warm tubs filled with bubbling salts, essences, and oils. My coffers are stocked with medicinal blends from secret rain forest plants imported from a world known to only a few.

For the tired, my domains of rest are as soothing as can be found. Ancient chants and mystical lullabies evoke sacred dreams to further assist my dreamers on their journeys.

As I constantly marvel at the dissimilarity of the voyagers who stay on, I am equally awed by the common desires for titillating tales, full bellies, and the pleasure of a warm bed. All are welcome within my walls, for I am the watcher, and I am forever the source of unity, diversity, abundance, and peace.

The Space Station represents a state of integration and unity. It is the symbol of the collective and the primal source.

The energy of this card can be expressed as the quality of the dominion we have within our reality—the degree of centered peace that marks our evolution into beings of compassionate detachment.

This paradoxical ability to be completely involved in every aspect of a creation while at the same time being serenely removed from the need for ego-driven outcome is the mark of the God and Goddess at our core. We are now operating in the realm of the "World Spirit"—the Christ Consciousness, the Buddha Nature, or any of the other so-called "nine billion names of God." This is the level of profound impact, unconditional love, and universal transmutation that shines forth when we release ourselves from all expectation and act as a living example of the Infinite Creator in whose image we are all cast.

This is also the level wherein we become completely aware of our own devils. By allowing as much light as possible to flow through us, we can either push away those inner demons or transform them into radiant, angelic aspects of our total selves. Without that light of complete self-truth, our loving God-Goddess energy can fall into megalomaniacal bestiality.

This card invites us to draw upon our infinite diversity in order to create a powerful unity within ourselves. We can then go forth in all that we do with our intentions and actions aligned in perfect harmony and balance.

STARS

CARD	ATTRIBUTE
Binary Stars	Synchronicity
Black Hole	Introspection
Comet	Signs/Cycles
Galaxy	Expansion
Nebula	Potential
Pulsar	Attention
Quasar	Cutting Edge
Red Giant	Completion
Supernova	Explosive Change
The Sun	Individuality
White Dwarf	Challenge
Wormhole	Connections

STARS

As we gaze up into the night sky, we see what appears to be a field of small, twinkling lights all about the same relative size and intensity. However, with the aid of telescopes and space probes, we know that stars are far from uniform and that many of those apparently single points of light are actually two, three, or more stars in proximity to one another. Stars range in size from dwarf stars, smaller than our moon and millions of times more dense, to red super giants bigger than the diameter of our entire solar system, to the crushing singularities of black holes, so small as to be virtually without size at all.

The dynamic life cycles of stars symbolize the cycles and outcomes of all the affairs of humans and every other being throughout the known universe.

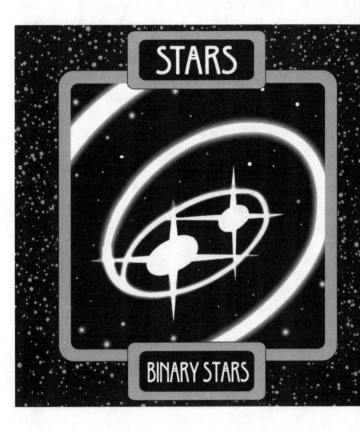
STARS

BINARY STARS

BINARY STARS

Cobalt and Crimson danced and spun around each other in slow, lazy spirals. Cobalt, the blue-white star, traced a glittering trail of stardust as he swung around and around with Crimson, his smaller reddish companion.

Together their combined wisps of solar wind mingled into a beautiful pinwheel of scintillating violet.

Cobalt and Crimson loved their dance and each other as much as they loved their single planetary offspring, Topaz, which orbited about them both. Topaz was a beautiful golden world wrapped in a thick, protective atmosphere whose radiant reflected light always signaled its whereabouts to its watchful parents.

Cobalt was much larger than Crimson, but they were well balanced in their stellar ballet, an impeccably timed choreography of cosmic proportions. Though they had been a pair for as long as they could remember, they had both seen star systems being born and fading to extinction all around them. Therefore, the couple knew better than to take each other for granted and so respected and cherished their differences as well as their similarities.

Then one day, a small moon named Ash wandered into their sphere of awareness. The poor planetoid was rocky and cold. Her protective instinct triggered, Crimson quickly queried the lost youngling as to the whereabouts of its mother.

The little moon said it had once been a member of a large family of planets that orbited a beautiful white star. But one day the mother star became sick and exploded in a violent eruption, flinging her children away and scattering them throughout the universe.

Cobalt, Crimson, and their golden child, Topaz, felt sorry for the forlorn little moon and were moved by its tragic tale. The family agreed that the orphaned moon needed a new home. The golden planet was overjoyed to have a new brother and invited Ash to orbit his gilt-flecked clouds.

The two parent stars continued their dance, celebrating the addition to their family, and their native son was proud to have his own companion. He grew up to be just like his mother and father, he and the adopted moon spinning happily around each other for the rest of their days.

On one level the Binary Stars card symbolizes the dynamics that often appear in relationships and families. Yet a higher quality of this energy reflects how polarities can enhance and complement one another and bring about a third dynamic that is more than just the sum of the first two.

This is the sign of synergy and balanced growth—that magnetic attraction of yin and yang that transcends our additive qualities and logarithmically elevates us to a new vista that neither single component is capable of carrying us to on its own.

However, even in partnership we must be self-empowered individuals so we can give to each other equally. If we lack belief in ourselves, this symbiotic interaction can become a prison of codependency with little chance for parole.

From a perspective of individual freedom and enlightened self-empowerment, all participants within our relationships can lend energy and support to all other members without fear of depletion or the draining demand to take responsibility for another's choices and challenges.

Rather than a top-heavy hierarchy that attempts to

control those of whom we assume ownership, a more evenly shared autonomy will allow us a greater range of creativity that will ultimately serve the greater good of everyone involved.

This is the card of cooperation and exchange between or among equals that energizes and inspires others to follow suit because of the obvious benefits we receive from such an egalitarian ideal.

The Binary Stars card also reflects the understanding that relationships exist so that each partner can see and learn about him- or herself by what is reflected by the other and grow as a result. This card may indicate the imminent arrival of a soul mate, but it also reminds us that if we haven't yet attracted the one we want to love, then we can best spend our time by loving the one we're with.

BLACK HOLE

The black hole was lost deep in concentration. He pondered and wondered and worried and wallowed within his thick cloak of darkness.

Other stars found him aloof and withdrawn. It's true that he pretty much kept to himself, but it wasn't his fault he had collapsed into this black introspection. That's just the way things were.

No matter how the other stars coaxed him, he couldn't seem to emerge from his weighty shell. The black hole still faintly remembered what it had been like to be a brightly burning star, and he had shone hotter than most. But now, that life was over.

One day, his great mass had come crashing in on itself with agonizing density. His days had dissolved into solitary singularity, with one moment no different from the next. And yet he felt the inward tug pulling him toward . . . he didn't know what, but he was consumed with the pressure of expectation and the promise of great potential.

Over and over, he reached out with his intense gravitic grip to pull stray comets and asteroids into his inescapable web. He hoped that they might satiate his need to know what was happening and help him to expand once again. However, all they did was add to his accelerating diminishment. Even light brought him no illumination. Depressed, he withdrew even further into his hermetical exile.

Finally, a tiny ray of hope sparked the very core of his consciousness. *Perhaps*, he proposed to himself, *the only way out is to go further into myself. I've been searching for answers from the outside and have received only darkness in return.*

Maybe the light I seek is at the end of my very own tunnel—
a passage to the other side of my being.

Though he was full of fear, the black hole knew what he must do. He ceased fighting against the inexorable pull within his soul and spiraled inward at a dizzying speed. In an instant, he collapsed into a single point and disappeared from the universe he called home.

In the next moment his awareness exploded outward into a new and wondrous space; he had crossed a threshold into another dimension of being. He looked at himself and beheld his miraculous metamorphosis into a white hole— an unending fountain of energy and light.

This reorganized self started filling the new universe with the essence of everything he had ever been, bursting forth in new combinations. Unlimited possibilities sprang into his awareness. As he expanded, becoming more ethereal with each ecstatic second, he knew that his acceptance of himself was the key that had allowed him to be reborn and convert his own darkness into glorious light.

If we have been drawn to the Black Hole card, it is time to weigh the gravity of our situation. There may be many crucial portions of ourselves or circumstances in our reality that have been hidden and must be explored.

The greatest depth within us is where our answers reside, and to truly know ourselves, we must venture into the center of our being. This may be a dark time, filled with morbid fears and deep doubts about who we are, why we are here, and what we're supposed to do.

Yet we are rewarded with the rainbow at the end of the storm. We are our own light, shining at the end of every self-made tunnel.

This card signifies great transition from our familiar concepts to as yet unrealized potential. However, this process can often seem to immobilize us in the cement of uncertainty. If we feel trapped, withdrawn, or depressed by the apparent collapse of our world, we can take heart that, quite often, the road to salvation is in the direction we are being pulled. Instead of resisting our inward plunge, we may redefine our depression as compression—that intense, creative imperative that forces us to rethink all that we know and helps us emerge from our black cocoon completely reborn.

Though our passage through our "dark night of the soul" may cut our ties to the rest of the world, the depth of such solitude is sometimes necessary in order to heal the sorrow that lies buried under the weight of decades of denial. We are comforted by the fact that the universe is infinite in an inward direction as well as an outward one, so that even in the face of death there will always be the promise of rebirth.

COMET

"**H**aven't I seen you somewhere before?" the comet teased as she flew swiftly past the Moon.

"Haven't I heard that joke before?" the Moon teased back.

The comet always shared the same joke each time she returned to the inner solar system, which she had done thousands of times.

"You travel farther out in your orbit than do the planets in your system," the Moon noted. "Don't you ever hear any new jokes out there?"

"I like consistency," the comet explained. "Besides, look who's talking. You orbit the same planet month after month and go around the Sun like clockwork year after year. You hardly ever have anything new to tell me."

"Exactly my point," stressed the Moon. "I always see the same old things. I look forward to your visits so you can bring me news about what's going on in the rest of the system. By the way, your tail is as beautiful as always."

"Thank you," the comet gushed. "It is quite bright, isn't it? I think the Sun is melting a few more ice pockets on my body than usual, leaving an extremely long trail this time—over three million miles—and it's especially effervescent. I left all the other comets in a tailspin! I think they're quite jealous."

"Now, that's news," encouraged the Moon. "Any other juicy gossip?"

"Well, you know my good friend recently had an impactful encounter. She dove headfirst into Jupiter and broke into twenty-one pieces. It was quite a show!"

"I heard about that," said the Moon. "You comets certainly have flair."

"Things won't be the same without her, but I guess she felt it was time for a change. Never a dull moment out there."

"I understand," the Moon sympathized. "You see so many new sights on your journey, you're never sure what you'll find each time around. You actually envy my monotonous existence, don't you?"

"It would be nice to have some predictability," sighed the comet. "Why, I never even get to see you every time I come in this close because I rarely retrace the exact same path.

"There is always the Sun, of course. He seems steady enough. And Mercury . . . that fellow's always in retrograde. Perhaps I should be grateful for my vagabond nature. Well, I must be off now."

The Moon acknowledged the comet's departure. "I know. I could see your tail brightening even as we spoke. The Sun has quite an effect on you."

"I hope we get to visit next time around," ventured the comet as she sped off toward her heliocentric rendezvous.

"Until we meet again," said the Moon. "You know where to find me."

The comet flared through space—a small celestial arrow fletched with feathers of light.

"Haven't I seen you somewhere before?"

The planet Venus recognized the playful question as the comet approached, just as it had thousands of times before.

In the Comet card, there is an interesting and unusual quality: it represents cycles of occurrences, but not exact repetition. This is the energy of the wanderer, the nomad.

The Comet also reflects important cycles within our collective consciousness as we spiral up the evolutionary chain, repeating our history in many general ways, but never quite exactly.

Comets are the signposts of the heavens, the symbol of news and telltale signs of imminent events. They catch our attention and, by their synchronous timing, point out the aspects of our collective social dynamics that will be prominent in the upcoming cycle of growth. Long heralded as portents of doom, comets simply underline concepts that we have often dreaded to contemplate, and thus we blame the messenger for delivering news we are loath to hear.

Comet energy can sometimes symbolize a short attention span and an inability to stay focused on or committed to one idea. They can also reveal personalities that on one level may appear to shine, but really contain very little more than a flashy disposition.

The qualities of the Comet may impart a sense of déja vu, the feeling that we have been this way before. However, this is a reflection that is one step beyond rote repetition, as it brings with it a quality of mystery that invites us to explore out beyond the fringes of the familiar.

GALAXY

Can you guess who I am?

Pools of raw energy within me dream of taking form, and I urge them to do so with creative abandon.

Nebulas of gas and stardust are the rich wellsprings that forever quench my insatiable desire to become more.

Meteors shower their splendor upon the eager faces of my planetary dwellers, while pulsars play their tunes in rhythmic light rays to a star-studded audience. Within my twilight, red giants reminisce of kingdoms that have come and gone, while young stars radiate wonder of futures yet in store.

My quasars' brilliance baffles the brightest observers when they streak by, leaving only curiosity in their trails. Even I am astounded by their velocity!

Ships flicker like fireflies within my borders, pollinating myriad worlds with the seeds of creation. They are the keepers of my garden.

Blazing suns set on multitudinous horizons, counting off the grains of sand in the hourglass of my life, while supernovas explode in great bursts, sending dying embers to become the sparks of new life . . . and I ponder the next surprise.

I am so vast I can never really know myself completely. I am in a constant state of becoming, ever expanding and unmeasurable . . .

Can you guess who I am?

The spiral is the symbol of growth along lines of expansion. It represents the upward evolutionary pattern that influences the path and the outcome of each and every thought, word, and deed—every mountain, bird, and seed within nature.

If the Galaxy card has spiraled into our space, it is a message to celebrate: our universe is in the proper position for total manifestation of all our dreams, requiring only the slightest push to set things in motion. Once begun, this energy has a life of its own, and with each cycle it gathers more momentum and takes on more dynamic qualities and potential for new developments.

However, we must be cautious and not become too blasé in our easy success. Otherwise, our heads may spin with shallow conceit, landing us in a downward spiral of narcissistic impotence and ignorance.

We contain the pearls of our own wisdom and the seeds of our own destruction. The symbol of the spiral represents the irresistible force that will carry us in whatever direction we have set our sights.

Such force is a great power, for the Galaxy is like a gear, enmeshed with all other galactic gears by its gravitational teeth. We know that the turning of any single gear will always turn all others, and by this fact we can humbly realize that a change made in one part of the universe makes a difference throughout all creation.

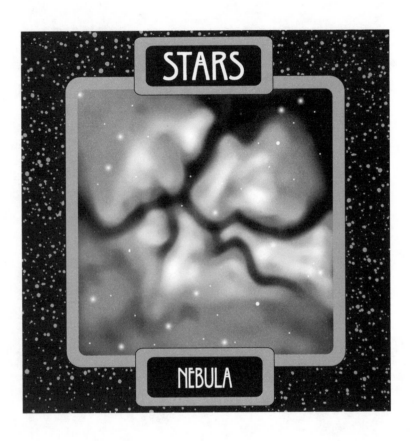

STARS

NEBULA

NEBULA

Why don't the galaxies leave me alone? They are always asking me when I intend to grow up. Well, the fact is, I think they're all envious of my freedom and youth.

I've heard comments whispered behind my back: "That nebula is lazy and confused." Not so! I'm simply so full of potential that I need to take plenty of time to consider every possibility I may become . . . I mean, I don't want to make any rash decisions now, do I?

Some say I'm unorganized. How preposterous. I know where all my parts are. Just because I leave them to roam freely, unencumbered by form, doesn't mean I'm scattered . . . does it?

They can call me immature if they wish, but I happen to like being me and I prefer to think of myself as pure potential. I mean, what's the hurry? I'll grow up, evolve into star systems and have planets to watch over for who knows how long. Then what's left? Growing old, burning out, collapsing into darkness . . . What's the rush?

And what do they mean, I can't know who I am when I remain clouded by indecision? Wrong again. I know exactly who I am. I'm 99 percent hydrogen and helium, with minute percentages of other gases and a tiny bit of icy cosmic dust—the interstellar medium from which the universe is formed. So what's the problem?

I've been told that my very name has been used to refer to something that is unclear and indistinct. Well, sticks and stones would break my bones if I had any, but names mean very little to me. I refuse to be confined by a label. Call me what you will, but I'll just keep changing. I'm nowhere near being finished exploring new configurations.

I'm in the prime of my life, and though I'm young, I'm not stupid. I'm going to make these carefree years last and last . . . I relish the idea of spending the hours floating in the sea of my essence, free from commitment, pondering the marvelous probable futures I may someday enjoy—if I ever decide to make up my mind!

The Nebula card very clearly cautions us that it may be premature to act too quickly. When we become excited by the prospect of some promise of fulfillment, we can often act rashly, initiating things that are simply not ready to be pushed ahead.

Inception is its own state of being, and we need not devalue it by assuming it is only an unformed and worthless precursor to a more important expression. If we do not allow the ingredients in our cosmic soup to steep and simmer according to the required recipe, we will wind up sipping a thin, tasteless concoction.

We might assume that this card is asking us to be patient, but what it is really saying is that if we allow whatever exists in the moment to be just as meaningful as what will come later, then we won't really need patience, as our full attention will be absorbed in the here and now. Waiting for something "better" diminishes the worth of what is right in front of us, and so we fail to extract the critical information that would actually help us move on toward completion.

We must appreciate the potential in all our undertakings. This is a perfect time to prepare, to plan, to organize, and to lay the foundation that can handle the scope of our dreams and visions.

As with most energies, Nebula sometimes contains dark matter that can act to obscure our sight and diffuse our ambition, leaving us to wallow in a quagmire of procrastination. It is usually our negative definitions that cloud our issues. If this is the case, taking some time to clarify our beliefs can help our nebulous confusion resolve into shining stars of inspiration.

STARS

PULSAR

PULSAR

The little blue pulsar spun through the vast emptiness of space, flashing and rotating its light beams like a lonely lighthouse on a remote and desolate shore.

Why am I all alone? he wondered. *Why do I never meet others like me? Please, all knowing Creator, can you tell me?*

The Creator spoke with the little pulsar and said, "Do not be lonely, little one. You are very important to me, and so I have a very important job for you to do." The Creator told the pulsar he must gather all his energy and project his light beams as far as possible, so he could get a message to someone at a great distance who needed help.

The little blue pulsar was very pleased to have been chosen by the Creator for this important task. He spun as fast as he could and sent his beams farther into space than ever before. After a long while, the pulsar was exhausted. He slowed down and rested his weary beams.

"Why have you stopped?" asked the Creator."

"I am very tired," the little pulsar complained. "Besides, no one has answered the message. I don't know if I am strong enough to do as you ask."

"I know you can do it," the Creator assured him. "I have faith in you. You're much more powerful than you think you are. If you persevere, I know you will succeed."

Uplifted by the Creator's faith in him, the little blue pulsar focused all his will, all his intention, and all his heart. He spun faster and faster, until he became a little blue blur. With one ecstatic burst, he flung his light beams so far out into the universe that he couldn't tell how far they went.

"That's the spirit!" encouraged the Creator. "You're the brightest little pulsar there is."

The little pulsing star was so happy and felt so light that he just kept on spinning and shining. He even forgot he was alone.

Suddenly, he saw something. A faint light flickered and pulsed in the distance. It was similar to his own, but with one important difference: this light was pink.

His heart leapt! A pink pulsar! He wasn't alone after all! Now he understood what the Creator had done. He had tricked the little pulsar into thinking someone else had needed help, when, of course, he was the one who had been helped. The little pulsar's willingness to aid someone else turned out to be the greatest gift to himself.

By reaching out, by shining as brightly as he could, the little blue pulsar had been able to let the other pulsar know where he was. He spent the rest of his days in joy, his own blue beams and those of the little pink pulsar caressing and dancing together in a sky full of brilliant stars.

When the Pulsar announces its presence, we can be assured that important events are about to reveal themselves in our lives.

This is also the energy that heralds an imminent breakthrough to a new level of interaction, either internally or externally, or signals that we are on the verge of being recognized, celebrated, or honored for our accomplishments. Much public attention can follow as new situations unfold, and this may be the time to get in touch with how best to handle the fame and scrutiny that often accompany those who stand in the spotlight.

In another context, this card can be a cry for attention, from ourselves or from others. On the positive side, this can be answered by compassionately acknowledging those who feel lost in the dark. On the negative side, the need to be noticed can represent the habits of self-aggrandizing personalities who feed their egos on a diet of flattery and shallow compliments.

Within this symbol is also the quality of impulsive behavior with its flashing beacon. This is a warning sign of unseen difficulties on the path ahead that need to be illuminated before we can proceed.

With regard to public interaction, the pulsar reveals that as we make it our goal to be of service to others, we ourselves will always be rewarded in kind.

Like lighthouses, we can send our beacons into the night, helping others to avoid the dangerous waters of depression and self-doubt. With our hands firmly on society's pulse, we can know how to respond in the most constructive and beneficial manner for all, including ourselves.

Perhaps most significantly, the Pulsar urges us to believe in ourselves with unshakable faith. It encourages us to reach farther than we now believe possible and to truly shine by pushing through our fears and doubts and taking the necessary actions to realize our visions.

Drawing this card is a sign that we have untapped inner strength. We must pull ourselves up out of martyrdom and the victim mentality; drop our "poor me" attitude; stand straight and tall, stand out in a crowd, stand up for our truths—in other words, just do it!

QUASAR

Of all the things in this expanding universe, only light itself is swifter than I. I am not a star, though from a great distance I may appear to be. I burn more brightly than a billion suns. I am a quasar on the edge of known space, first to arrive while the stars and planets follow far behind.

At a rate of 91 percent of the speed of light, I am still able to receive information about the goings-on of my slower siblings. They all regard me with a certain awe and try their best to learn more of what I am. Some planets have even wagered their rings, betting they can find some way to approach my distant realm and come to know me.

They sometimes coax the comets to swing wider in their far-flung orbits in the hope of glimpsing a secret or two of mine, but these are futile attempts. If they could reach where I am now, by the time they'd arrive I'd be somewhere else. Even the light that reveals my presence to them is thirteen billion years old, so they never see me as I am, but only as I was when the universe was new.

To be honest, I am moving so fast I can't slow down to take a look at myself, so I am as mystified by my essence as all the rest. The only things known of me are my existence and the names used to identify me.

In one quadrant of the universe, I am called the Luminous One; in another I am known as the "fire of the gods." But I am most fond of the identity bequeathed upon me by a quaint little world called Earth. There I am simply known as OQ172—a number and nothing more. I find this numerical appellation fitting and proper to one of my exalted station, for the name does not assume to know anything about me . . . it only tells them that I am here.

Light and the Infinite are my only companions on this voyage, for I am a quasar, destined to go where nothing and no one has ever gone before.

The Quasar has no time to rest on its laurels. This energy is up at the crack of dawn and has done more by noon than most do in a day.

While this great energy can inspire us and allow us to accomplish a great deal, this card is also warning us not to run away with ourselves. All too often, we keep ourselves busy as a means of avoiding relationships or other important responsibilities and even of declining to get to know ourselves. We simply become a blur of activity with no real identity.

But the speed of the Quasar can place us on the cutting edge of whatever we decide to do. It impels us to excel at our task, finding innovative ways to approach a challenge that would daunt others, and to break new ground and be the first to see unlimited possibilities where most would give up.

The Quasar energy has no time for excuses, and if not gifted with grace, we might be perceived as abrupt, blunt, or even downright rude. Being first in many areas does often depend on a direct, no-nonsense attitude, yet maintaining a humble and loving demeanor will help temper this sometimes abrasive behavior into a more refreshing and welcome honesty that instantly clarifies the situation.

This card is the mirror that reminds us that we are made of light and have virtually unlimited potential. We are able to initiate great adventures that can propel us far beyond our restrictive assumptions of our capabilities and of what there is to find once we cross the lines of convention set by less-imaginative souls.

Bringing the Quasar card to light can signal that we are ready for that flash of insight, that gestalt of total awareness that allows us to see all things in creation in relation to everything else. But we must remember that such insight comes only with proper focus and perspective.

It is said that chance favors the prepared mind. This really means that when we create a solid foundation of information by learning about the things that interest us, synchronicity is generated. We will automatically be at the right place and time to receive the gifts from the Infinite that we truly need to live a rich, fulfilling life.

STARS

RED GIANT

RED GIANT

"Tell us another story, Granddad," the young stars sang in unison.

Rusty, the old red-giant star, rippled his ruddy corona in smug satisfaction. He enjoyed recounting tales from his rich long life, and the novice stars never seemed to tire of hearing them.

"Three of my worlds once teemed with life," he proudly began. "When I was a young yellow star, oh, about five billion years ago, my golden aura nurtured those civilizations until they matured into beautiful, spacefaring beings. Of course, as I grew older, they went off to live around younger stars like yourselves, but I didn't mind."

The ancient star grew silent as he slipped into self-reflection. Some of the newer stars grew impatient with Rusty's reveries, but most were content to wait two or three hundred thousand years until the old star remembered his eager audience.

"Beginnings and endings are good things," the old one finally whispered. "Both are so clearly defined. Sometimes I get a little confused about what happened in between, but when it comes to completion, I know exactly where things stand."

"What do you mean, Granddad?"

Rusty favored the youthful star Glimmer with an affectionate, rumbling laugh. "You'll understand when you're as old as I am. For now, just enjoy the fact that everything is new and exciting."

With that, Rusty drifted into reminiscence once again. He remained in that dreamlike state longer and longer each time. The physical universe held little mystery for him now. He focused his wizened mind inward, cooled and darkened just a bit more, and contemplated what he might discover as he faded into the great beyond.

The Red Giant speaks about the endings of things. Now is the time for us to slow down and turn our attention to the last-minute details, making sure that everything is in its proper place and that there are no loose ends or unfinished business before we move on to our next opportunity.

From the point of view of this energy, we are given the chance to gain perspective: to look back upon our experiences and use the knowledge we have accumulated to take us forward. It can also allow us the wisdom to see what other paths might have been taken and to share this insight with those who might benefit from such illumination.

If we are holding on to something that no longer serves us or to things we know cannot be changed, it is time for us to let them go. Otherwise, our inner light can fade to a smoldering ember of regret. Rather, our memories can be cherished, as each endeavor is a unique statement in creation, never to be repeated throughout eternity.

This card can bring past lives to light so that we can see how long-term cycles may be connected to present events. In addition, this might be the time to seek the wisdom of our elders, whether in the flesh, in spirit, or even a symbolic, archetypal grandparent in order to learn from their experience.

When we are lulled into reverie and reflection, it is important that we do not wind up living in the past. Instead, we can meditate on our ancient heritage, and while we may still have far to go, we can marvel on how far we have already come.

STARS

SUPERNOVA

SUPERNOVA

The pressure was intense. Starbright wasn't sure he could stand it for much longer. He began to question his decision to change and wondered if the other stars had been right.

"Slow down," they had urged. "Take your time," they beseeched him. "What's your hurry?" they constantly queried.

But Starbright hadn't been happy lately. He was bored with the slow, steady shine that was typical of his stellar soul mates. He wanted to be something more—to do something . . . astonishing.

He had burned with consistent dependability for ten billion years, shedding his light and providing warmth for his planetary progeny. But now they were gone, having collided with asteroids or simply cooled their molten cores until they were nothing more than lifeless rocks floating in empty space. There was no motivation for Starbright to continue such a boring existence.

He loved his life, though, and didn't wish to merely fade away as so many other stars did. No, he wanted to be useful again somehow; he wanted to make a difference. So he had accelerated his internal fires until his desire for change had become an all-consuming passion that filled him with an unbearable pressure to grow, to expand, to explode into something new.

With a shocking epiphany of illumination, Starbright detonated into a coruscating chaotic bubble of stellar dust. Glittering gases spread through the void, churning and frothing and mixing with abandon. With newly transcendent awareness he realized what he had become: the raw primal essence from which new stars and planets would eventually be born.

Though no longer a star, Starbright's life had meaning once again. Wrapping himself in the warmth of renewal, he drifted into a deep sleep where he could dream of his promising tomorrows.

Everyone stand back . . . the energy of this card is explosive! The Supernova bursts upon our awareness as the symbol of rapid and total change.

This card puts us in touch with the volatile nature of events that can seem random and unexpected, but which may have been brewing beneath the surface for some time.

Individuals and endeavors containing this energy can shift at a moment's notice, crossing the threshold into acceleration, completion, or chaos.

Within this vibration, we can accomplish miraculous changes in the wink of an eye. We can inspire new probabilities and modes of thought through bursts of creativity.

If not directed by positive influences, however, this frenetic capacity can pressure us into explosively destructive behavior and fits of uncontrolled rage.

It is also said that the brightest stars burn the quickest, and this can have light or dark connotations. On one side, a single ecstatic explosion may be preferable to several more mundane experiences. On the other side, living hard and fast can burn us out before we realize our full potential.

The Supernova snaps us to attention and prompts us to make those needed changes or to be on the alert for an abrupt restructuring of events. Things are reaching critical mass, and if we don't attend to business, our world can come apart at the seams.

We don't need to panic, however. Just as order can break down into chaos, chaos possesses a hidden underlying order. It is sometimes necessary to allow our old reality to break down so that we can make room for a new breakthrough.

STARS

THE SUN

THE SUN

Dear Children,

I'm beaming you this message because I've been very busy, and I know I haven't communicated with each of you as often as a father should. There is so much responsibility that comes with my work as the Sun. I love my job, but I wouldn't wish it on any of you. Be happy that you are planets, with no task greater than to stay in your own orbits and avoid colliding with the occasional asteroid.

Quite often, the pressure of my station will stoke my anger and my temper will flare. I do not mean to take it out on you, my children, though I know there have been times when you have felt the heat of my wrath.

Especially you, Mercury, my little brave boy who is so close to my heart yet is always speeding to and fro: It has been so long since I was young that I forget how exuberant children are. You can be most vexing, but I love you nonetheless.

Venus, my daughter: You are so like your father in your hot-blooded passion for life.

Earth, my precious jewel, so like your sister and yet so cool: You have taken the gift of my light and loving warmth and blossomed with miraculous life. I know you are sometimes sickly and sad, but I believe that someday you will shine in your own way as brightly as I do in mine.

Mars, my precocious son—rough and tumble, always ready for a fight: I see that you sometimes distance yourself from me and so run hot and cold within our relationship. Yet you will always be my little soldier, and I know that with my guidance and your strength, our love will be rekindled.

Jupiter, my scion, my elder child: Many a night you have wished you could be a star like me. Alas, you haven't the mass to shine, nor are you the center of this family. But take heart . . . your pet moons orbit about you and need your devotion, just as I am devoted to supporting all of you.

Saturn, my princess, my wildest daughter: As you so lovingly reflect my light in your halo, you are truly the twinkle in your father's eye. Whenever I am beset by the black spots of my dark, brooding doubts, I gaze upon you and am renewed.

Chiron . . . my littlest child: What can I say to you? I feel your pain, being so small between your grander siblings. But you are important to me, for you are the link—the bridge that balances Saturn's worldly ways and Uranus's psychic introspection.

Uranus and Neptune, my twins: Though you were born of my fire, you have become the sojourners into the liquid mysteries that lead our family toward deeper knowledge.

Pluto, my lonely child: Little of my love reaches your soul, and while I am the core of life, you search instead for the threshold between the security of our home and the cold, forsaken depths of the unknown. I can only send my love and wish you well.

My children, I have in my time been worshiped and cursed, gentle and harsh, smoldering and ablaze. Though once I seemed the all-important center of your existence and have now been delegated to the status of an insignificant speck in the pantheon of the heavens, there is one thing I give you that will never change. I will love and support whatever you choose to be until my life dims to a final, dying ember of my nurturing solar flame.

Your loving father, the Sun

The Sun defines not only the idea of male or father ener-gy, but it extends into the concept of being an individual and recognizing or being recognized for the personal quali-ties that make us unique.

The message being given here is for us to bask in the light that reveals our special attributes and to find security in simply being who we are. In this context, self-expression does not have to represent a negatively inflated ego, but is simply the acknowledgment of the ego's natural capacity to keep us focused on our singularly unique path in life.

The Sun card radiates a willingness and a will to share our individual reasons for being. There is an understanding that in order for the world to receive our gifts, we some-times must take center stage without fear and stand boldly in the spotlight. If we cannot accept and express our true, radiant selves as deserving of a chance to shine, then we may be eclipsed by those around us or by belief systems we have accepted that are not representative of our own truth. We must be ourselves in the here and now: Time waits for no one.

We all have our day in the sun. This card sends a beam to help illuminate our truth and awakens us to our position in the scheme of things. We must act while there is still enough light for our treasures to sparkle, or we may go into the nighttime of our lives laden with regret.

STARS

WHITE DWARF

WHITE DWARF

The diminutive star was frozen in a quandary of polarized revelations. It was once a great effulgent star, but it had shrunk to the size of a small moon and emitted only a weak, sickly glow. Previously a regal conflagration of nuclear fire, it now floated through its own ashes like a dying ember—a thick, dense cinder of impenetrable neutronium.

Yet while it contemplated its fall from grace, the white dwarf recognized the paradox in its plight. Being composed of the densest matter, the small star now had an unimaginably powerful aura of gravity that swept up all minor matter in its path, adding it to its own massive presence.

The star was frustrated by its inability to shine, but saw the advantage to unobtrusively gathering the glistening particulates of its former incarnation and converting them into a new smooth shell of crystalline armor. Whereas previously its light had shone far and wide, the white dwarf realized that this had been but a showy display compared to the substance it now possessed. It had pull; it had weight—it was a force to be reckoned with.

But while it considered these portentous matters, polarity still resonated deep within its soul. The white dwarf knew that in order for it to exercise its newfound power, it must remain in balance. With great concentration and diligence, it ultimately developed a finely tuned neutrality that forever suspended it between the microcosmic spark of the atom and the imponderable enormity of the Infinite.

When this card creeps into our lives, we may find things are slow going. This is the energy of a thick, dense reality where the least little idea is subjected to interminable analysis and endless pondering, if anything gets done at all.

If the White Dwarf is sitting in our path, we may meet with great resistance and experience overwhelming frustration in our attempts to get things moving. This card may mean we are bogged down with flat, uninspired, unhealthy, outdated, or fatalistic definitions about what things mean and how we interpret the events that surround us.

On a slightly lighter side, the White Dwarf can auger the presence of a matter of great weight and consequence, which can profoundly affect our lives or those of the beings around us. If so, we must take care to weigh all the issues, perspectives, and potential results so that our decision does not produce an unstable outcome. The White Dwarf symbol is the epitome of the phrase "When the going gets tough, the tough get going."

WORMHOLE

"Just one moment, please, and I'll connect you."

Today was a busy day for the wormhole. There seemed to be more messages than usual passing from one star to the next, and without the shortcut the wormhole provided through space, those messages would take years to reach their destinations rather than mere moments.

Though the wormhole wasn't a star, a planet, or any kind of object one could view through a telescope, it was the connecting link between remote regions of the universe. It served as the bridge joining the island galaxies that dotted the infinite ocean of time and space.

At either end, the tunnel-shaped wormhole was a simple whirlpool of energy—a rotating entry to the interstellar highway. But inside, the swirling tube became a gateway to all points in creation, both anywhere and anywhen. Past, present, and future were all the same within the wormhole; a star a billion light-years away was just a second's jaunt.

The wormhole's multidimensional branchings pulsed from the voluminous flow of information being directed through them. The stalwart channel bent gravity this way and that like a musical virtuoso, expertly directing each message, ray of light, or spacecraft to its appropriate exit portal.

"I haven't been this busy since those two galaxies collided in sector 3000," mused the wormhole. If it hadn't been for the wormhole's skill at balancing the flood of gravity waves that resulted from that disaster, the fabric of space would have been seriously, perhaps irreparably, warped.

Suddenly, the wormhole was bombarded with simultaneous messages from all directions. They poured into its spinning funnel as gamma rays, x-rays, visible light, radio waves, and even whole fleets of spacecraft.

"What in creation could be happening?" wondered the besieged wormhole as it frantically juggled the barrage of radiation. Slowly, as it sorted the signals out, the wormhole realized that none of them had any destination codes; all the messages were intended for the wormhole itself.

"Congratulations!" they reverberated in unison. "We all want to thank you for your tireless service in uniting the universe. Without you we could not share, blend, and grow. We would like to honor you with the universal diplomatic award."

The wormhole was bathed in a glow of appreciation and gratitude. Nearly bursting with pride, it accepted the gracious gift of light and extended its connecting tunnels farther than ever before, bringing everyone throughout the vastness of existence just a little bit closer together.

The Wormhole card taps us into the energy of networking and forming connections. Under this guidance, we can more easily make associations between people, places, and things that would otherwise remain separated by time, space, or conceptual differences. This is the card of the catalyst—that state in which we can allow important events to manifest without necessarily being prominently involved ourselves.

This is the symbol of the diplomat, the negotiator, and the entrepreneur—all those with the skill and vision to cut through the red tape or see the potential outcome that could result from new alliances and arrangements of information.

However, we must be watchful not to scatter ourselves

too thin by taking on more than we really need to handle. Making connections requires very little coaxing when the timing is appropriate and the benefits are clear. We do not need to force or otherwise engineer factors into position; we need but correctly set the stage and the actors will appear.

Though *what we know* is an essential ingredient in success, there is truth to the adage that it's *who we know* that really counts. This does not mean we must become obsequious name-droppers, but that it is important to cultivate relationships that can become vital resources in the equation of manifestation. This way, we also allow those with talents and gifts to be of service while we reciprocate by acting as a resource for them in turn.

Finally, it is important for us to recognize the need for strengthening the connections within ourselves. We need to expand the link between the conscious and the unconscious and between our physical personalities and our farseeing higher selves.

PLANETS

CARD	ATTRIBUTE
Sol 1: Mercury	Messages
Sol 2: Venus	Love
Sol 3: Earth/Moon	Nature
Sol 4: Mars	War
Sol 5: Maldek	Destruction
Sol 6: Jupiter	Administration
Sol 7: Saturn	Wisdom
Sol 8: Chiron	Transition
Sol 9: Uranus	Unconscious
Sol 10: Neptune	Imagination/ Emotion
Sol 11: Pluto	Transformation
Sol 12: Nibiru	Mystery

PLANETS

The planet cards are based on our own solar system in order to bring the extraterrestrial energies in Contact Cards into balance with our human dynamics. Each planet or celestial body carries the familiar astrological or sociological meanings it has held for millennia as archetypal patterns and reflections on both the personal and collective levels.

Log of the survey ship Wanderer.
Excerpt from the survey of the Sol star system:

In every star system we survey that contains indigenous life on one or more of the planets, we always endeavor to use the names that the natives have bestowed upon their own system as a mark of respect. Therefore, after scanning the third planet outward from the central star, we find the proper name of that sun to be "Sol." As such, in our survey log we will refer to each world not only by its archetypal name, for example, "Earth," but also by its numerical position relative to the sun, for instance, "Sol 3," for the purpose of clarity.

Additionally, we will use our standard survey technique within these reports, which records both the physical and energetic archetypal characteristics of each planet in the system. We believe this will provide the deepest possible insight into the collective consciousness matrix of the Sol system's inhabitants.

SOL I:
MERCURY

Log of the survey ship Wanderer.
Excerpt from the survey of the Sol star system:

This small, rocky planet orbits very close to its parent star. Its unusual rotation would, from a viewpoint upon the surface, make the sun appear to rise, hang suspended in the sky, then set, repeating this strange movement twice each day.

From a symbolic perspective, this double dose of daily sunlight makes Mercury twice blessed. It can be considered especially favored by Sol in that Mercury attracts the sun's attention twice as often as any other world.

We intuit with our psychotronic scanners that Mercury chiefly represents speed and communication. This is substantiated by its unique communion with and its rapid orbit around Sol. This communication connection would extend to all methods by which information is accessed, including the psychic arts and the tools, such as crystal spheres and divining cards, that are associated with them.

Mercury's energy influences the elemental realm through the liquid metal quicksilver. Like this substance, this planet can symbolize elusiveness and the appropriately "mercurial" mood swings exhibited by individuals who are sensitive to high-frequency energies.

As viewed from Earth, Mercury's penchant for retrograde rotation adds to the probability of shifts and fluctuations in all activities involving communication, travel, commerce, and other forms of information exchange. This would also include the transmission and processing of thoughts along the body's nerve network and within the brain.

Overall, the energy dynamic of the first planet within this system would seem to lay the foundation for sharing and trading ideas and inventions among all the local worlds and from the solar realm to neighboring stars.

The card of Mercury informs us that we may be about to receive an important message and that we need to remain open to the events that surround us in order to extract any significant meanings that are not immediately obvious.

Communication is a two-way street. As a result, this card may also be urging us to send that critical information, have that necessary discussion, or share our thoughts and feelings without further delay.

If there are shadow qualities present within the immediate situation, Mercury may also be telling us this may not be the best time to make that move, take that trip, or proceed with our plans. We would be better advised to wait until all factors once again come to light before moving forward.

Business affairs and any form of exchange are within the realm of this card. Care should be taken to insure that everyone has the same understanding within any agreements and that all such contracts are thorough and complete. We need to remember that attention to these fine points does not mean that trust is lacking, but rather that clarity is called for in all our communications.

PLANETS

VENUS

SOL 2:
VENUS

Log of the survey ship Wanderer.
Excerpt from the survey of the Sol star system:

Venus is a sizable world, practically the twin of Sol 3, or Earth, though completely unlike Earth in its temperament. This second planet from Sol is a sphere wrapped in enigmatic clouds that hide the surface from all but our most penetrating scanners.

Beneath that dioxide blanket is a suffocating atmosphere that, due to a marked "greenhouse effect," exceeds temperatures of 800 degrees. With such inhospitable readings as these, it was astonishing to discover, through psychotronic scans, that Venus is the archetypal essence of love and pleasure associated with the Goddess energy.

Upon further investigation, this association began to make sense when considering such attributes as burning passion, the consummation of strong erotic desires, and Venus's association with the element copper, a high conductor of heat.

The second planet rotates on its axis in the opposite direction from all of the other planets in this system, with the exception of Sol 9, Uranus. Perhaps this unexpected motion reflects how the feminine energy of the Goddess can approach creation from a different, sometimes polar-opposite, point of view than the masculine perspective. Also, since Venus symbolizes attraction, her orbit illustrates the axiom that opposites attract or that we are about to attract someone special into our lives.

It takes 243 Earth days for Venus to rotate once on its axis and nearly 225 Earth days for it to orbit Sol, making Venus's day longer than its year. This planet therefore symbolizes the languid and relaxed attitude appropriate to exotic tropical climes and the timeless quality of love. Shining brightly with Sol's reflected light, Venus also mirrors beauty in all its forms, especially the arts and social graces.

Negatively, the energy of Venus could manifest as overindulgence and laziness, perhaps even to the extent of jealously hoarding energy and wealth instead of allowing it to flow. However, the second planet seems to exert a greater influence in the direction of appreciation and inspiration, and if experienced in pure form, it is more likely to radiate a strong, lasting, and unconditionally loving light.

The powerful energy of Venus reflects all manifestations

of sensuality, both physically and aesthetically. It requires presence and balance when tapped, as it could become quite intoxicating, plunging us into wanton hedonism and vanity. Coupled with a mature appreciation, however, this energy can be effectively channeled into artistic expressions of great beauty and grace.

Venus can ignite the heat of passion within any endeavor or relationship. With positive intention, we can allow an incipient glow to bloom into radiance. However, if we succumb to the smoldering heat of jealousy and rage, we might cause our desires to spontaneously combust.

As Venus illustrates, we sometimes need to go against convention in order to shine. Great art, passionate poems, and epic love stories all stir our inner selves. We are inspired to feel alive and, quite often, to reach for something more in our lives. This impulse then causes us to attract new experi-

our lives. This impulse then causes us to attract new experiences and grow.

Overall, this card is a call to become comfortable with our physicalness and to open our senses to enrich ourselves and, through creative expression, enrich the lives of our fellow journeyers, especially those we love.

SOL 3:
EARTH/MOON

Log of the survey ship Wanderer.
Excerpt from the survey of the Sol star system:

As the near twin of Venus, Earth also radiates a magnetic Goddess wave of energy that extends even to its nearby lunar companion, thus symbolizing mother and daughter.

A vibrant world, full of life in a variety of forms, Earth is the only naturally inhabited planet in this solar system. However, some extraterrestrial races other than ourselves have created temporary bases on several of the system's moons, including Earth's.

There is abundant water on Earth, which reinforces the feminine qualities of birth and the supportive flow of emotion. It is responsible for the planet's wild cornucopia of vegetation as well.

Earth's seasons symbolize regeneration and the fertility of nature, reflected not only in the verdant fields and forests but also in the resplendent array of animal life. Each species represents an aspect of the world's collective consciousness.

Earth's companion moon, which the inhabitants call simply "Moon" or Luna, is relatively large in comparison to its parent planet, and it exerts a great influence upon terrestrial tides and temperaments. In fact, the Earth/Moon system could almost be considered a double planet, thus explaining why Earth's inhabitants exhibit both the light and dark sides of their souls.

Anyone living on Earth (or the Moon) would be in a

constant struggle to maintain balance, as they would be subject to the overwhelming polarized "tug of war" between Earth's physically oriented energy and the Moon's subconscious and psychic symbolism.

The metal gold is usually associated with Sol, which is a star. Among the planets, Earth inherits the honor of being associated with gold because that metal symbolizes the life force, and Earth is the planet of life in the Sol system. A succinct encapsulation of Earth's symbology could be expressed as the seed that bursts forth, transmuting the raw elements of nature into the material manifestation of life in all its diverse expressions.

Silver—gold's counterpart—is the metal that symbolizes all lunar activities and opens the doorway to the mysteries of mind and spirit as well as determining cycles of feminine power and arcane perception. Thus Earth and Moon are the day and night of nature respectively, forming a balance between the foundational, grounded Earth energy and the more ephemeral magnetism of the heavens.

The Earth/Moon card expresses the healing, nurturing power of nature and the Goddess energy.

If Earth is smiling upon us, we are fortunate indeed. It means that renewal and regeneration will attend our constant search for our true selves and, if we have faith, ultimately allow us to reach our dreams of paradise. If the Moon is exerting its influence on us, we are being invited to explore, expand, and rely on our intuitive senses.

This is the card of personal responsibility—not that we are responsible *for* others but that we are responsible *to* them and the world by being naturally who we are. When we resist or fight against our true nature, we spread our unhappiness through the world, creating pollution, famine, and disease, both physically and spiritually.

The Earth/Moon card implores us to tap the feminine energies of nature, to go within and emerge, as a flower blooms, with renewed appreciation for ourselves and all expressions of life. It is an acknowledgment that everything in the world—people, animals, plants, and rocks—is a reflection of some aspect of our collective soul. If we do not respect the diversity around us, we invalidate ourselves as well and will never find the unity and peace that we seek.

If we do our job as caretakers, we will be able to drink deeply and forever of life's abundance, without fear of lack. Nature works when we allow it to; there is enough for all when we live in balance with it.

Drawing the Earth/Moon card signifies that, since Earth is home to the human race, it is time to get our house in order by going to our center and beginning with a personal housecleaning. The Moon aspect reminds us that when we express our inner psychic talents, we are not simply humans engaged in the spiritual experience—we are also spirits engaged in the human experience.

SOL 4:
MARS

Log of the survey ship Wanderer.
Excerpt from the survey of the Sol star system:

The fourth planet in the Sol system has a concentrated intensity about it. The entire surface of Mars is covered by reddish dust and rock, the result of the oxidation of the iron that is the symbolic metal of this planet.

It is evident from the polar caps and certain riverbed-like markings that scar the planet that at one time, perhaps millions of years ago, Mars had free-flowing water. Exactly what happened to change that and what rendered Mars into the bleak desert world we now find is unclear.

It is possible that a barrage of meteors or comets might have scoured the planet's topography, blowing away the atmosphere and insuring that this little world would remain forever lifeless. This is an apt scenario, for our scanners associate Mars with the attributes of warfare, battle, and fiery emotional energy.

Mars possesses two diminutive moons, appropriately named Phobos, which means fear, and Deimos, which means panic. Certainly those qualities are ever present where war runs rampant. Also, our analysis shows that these two rocky chunks may have been created by the destruction of Sol 5 (Maldek) and subsequently attracted to the orbit of Mars. This seems appropriate, as the remnants of destruction always echo the aftermath of war.

Because it lacks a substantial atmosphere, Mars will

rapidly heat under the full light of Sol, but as soon as night's shadow falls, the world is plunged into bitter cold. The emotional or energetic analogy would reflect itself in extremes of temperament: one moment flooded with ferocity, the next by cold calculation.

On the positive side, if properly balanced by constructive, conscious intention, these qualities can be sublimated into action, protection, self-assertion, and initiative. We can assume from these observations that Mars would be a powerful catalyst for positive change as long as its darker expressions are kept in check.

Lastly, we have spotted the remnants of a civilization in the Cydonia region of the planet. The ruins appear to be a sphinxlike face of gigantic proportions in proximity to a cluster of roughly pyramidal structures. We sense there may be some ancient connection to similar structures on Sol 3, especially considering that the Earthly area where some of the oldest pyramids exist is called Cairo in the natives' tongue, a word that translates as "Mars."

Therefore, the fierce energy of the red planet could also be construed as an ancient pattern in need of transmutation to a more ethereal state.

The card of Mars is a double-edged sword. With virtue and gallant intention, we can wield it to cut through conflict and confusion with shining clarity; with fear or self-righteousness, we succeed only in bloodying ourselves on the point of our impotent rage.

We are warned to be on the lookout for old habits that constantly plunge us into war with ourselves and others. We are cautioned against blaming the world for our woes and never facing the deep-set anger frozen within us that causes our frustrating failure to change our lives in the ways we desire.

The warrior's path is a high calling, and when accepted without a negative emotional "charge," it can induce uncompromising clarity in all our encounters and cut through all obstacles, just as light vanquishes shadow.

The intensity and momentum of this energy can be focused to see things through from beginning to end—to wage a successful campaign and accomplish our goal.

Warriors know how to follow the path of least resistance, though if confronted with opposing beliefs, they are not afraid to match point for point. However, our views about competition are changing. While in the past our notion of conflict implied that for every winner there must be a loser, we now know that everyone loses if we do not uphold the principle of a "win-win" scenario, where the outcome serves the best for all concerned.

While possessing a connection to Earth, symbolized by the Martian and terrestrial sphinxes, Mars is also psychically and emotionally bonded with Venus, the planet of attraction, which counterpoints Mars's energy of aggression. In drawing the sword of Mars, we must be cautious not to forcefully pursue what we are attracted to, for the chase can become an alluring trap. We must allow the attraction to work its own magic if it is to have lasting meaning.

We are called to remember that if we feel the need to force our point of view upon someone for any reason, then we don't have faith that our beliefs have the power to make changes naturally. If so, we will quickly find ourselves championing a lost cause.

PLANETS

MALDEK

SOL 5:
MALDEK

(Asteroid Belt)

Log of the survey ship Wanderer.
Excerpt from the survey of the Sol star system:

This orbit is the site of a cosmic tragedy: the destruction of an ancient world that our psychotronic beams identify as Maldek. Only thousands of chunks of rocky debris now remain, circling Sol as though still attempting to retain planetary status.

Upon first encountering the belt, we thought the asteroids might represent a world that had never formed. However, by tracing many cometary orbits backward on our computers, we discovered that most of their trajectories began at the same spot within Maldek's orbit several million years ago.

By our calculations, it would appear that Maldek may have collided with another planetary body of some sort, possibly as that trespassing world charted an eccentric course through this system, leaving destruction in its wake. The combined asteroidal mass does not add up to form a world of sufficient size to occupy this orbit, so we suspect much of Maldek was scattered in all directions. The two Martian moons are nothing more than jagged chunks of rock, and we surmise they may be orphaned remnants of Maldek adopted by Martian gravity.

Of course, this interpretation does not have to be literal in the corporeal sense. It can simply portend a great shift in life from old patterns toward a new way of seeing that involves the symbolic death of the ego.

In any event, the fate of Maldek is a sobering reminder of the consequences of being unable, or unwilling, to change direction in the face of obvious danger.

However, if one survives such a cataclysm relatively intact, it does present an opportunity to begin anew.

Like the Tower card in a traditional tarot deck, Maldek symbolizes the tearing down or coming apart of events.

Though this card can mean we are caught in a downward spiral of self-destruction, it normally signifies that it is sometimes necessary for our plans to fall apart before we can finally see the naked path that would be best for us to take. Too much structure and rigidity, when we are faced with the inevitable tide of change, can cause our inflexible facades to snap and crumble, plummeting us into dark despair.

We must learn to bend like a sapling in the wind if we are to thrive. A complete spiritual, mental, emotional, and even physical inventory of our condition must be taken to assess our ability to adapt.

This card cautions that if our energy becomes too scattered, spinning off in too many directions at once, we must pull ourselves together. We need to become more cohesive and holistic in our approach or our dreams could shatter upon the rocks of our egotistical insistence.

Habits can sometimes be difficult to change. By allowing things to come crashing down, we can give ourselves a chance to clear away the debris and start over with a clean slate.

PLANETS

JUPITER

SOL 6:
JUPITER

Log of the survey ship Wanderer.
Excerpt from the survey of the Sol star system:

The entire survey team decided that one word describes Jupiter best: *immense!* We don't need to rely on psychotronic scans to know this is the "Lord of Worlds" in this system. In fact, our measurements reveal that if Jupiter had been slightly more massive in its original inception, it would likely have ignited into a companion star for Sol.

It is impressive nonetheless: a gigantic gaseous planet of churning, colored cloud bands and enormous cyclonic storms. The most notable of these titanic hurricanes, a great reddish spot, is easily three times the size of Earth, and all the remaining planets in the system could fit within Jupiter's expansive bulk.

Energetically, the sixth world is the symbol of knowledge and administration, of power and wisdom, although these attributes can quickly flip toward the self-righteous rigidity of a demagogue, maniacally corrupting the weak of will. Earth natives call such despots "tin-plated gods," and, thus, with regard to its dark potential, tin is the appropriate metal of Jupiter.

In summation, it can be seen that if Jupiter energy wishes to retain its balanced orbit, it must not throw its weight around. Rather, it needs to expand its influence through educated management of its considerable power and resources.

When the Jupiter card appears, announcing the planet's great presence, we are made aware of influential energies that organize all elements into their proper positions for power and success. Influences of this magnitude require an "oath of office" to insure that power is used responsibly and with integrity.

Absolute power will not corrupt absolutely unless the seeds of corruptible beliefs have already been planted within us. Only the purest conductor can carry the highest energy. Any elements not in perfect attunement will create resistance, leading to a complete meltdown and an inability to withstand the consequences of such discord.

This card instructs us to make wise use of all our resources and to remember that the proper delegation of power and responsibility is the mark of inspired orchestration. Trying to impose an egocentric control over every random factor indicates lack of faith in the conditions we have attracted that already contain the necessary ingredients for success. Maintaining a sure but light touch at the controls allows us to shift course at a moment's notice should our goals unexpectedly change.

The card of Jupiter holds the promise of great expansion, both of self and resources. It is a powerful sign that anything is possible. Only we can limit those possibilities by imposing too many restrictions on our limitless imaginations.

SOL 7:
SATURN

Log of the survey ship Wanderer.
Excerpt from the survey of the Sol star system:

Even though all the gas-giant planets in this system have rings, Sol 7, or Saturn, is adorned with the most magnificent rings this survey team has ever encountered. The millions of chunks of ice that form the rings glitter like crystal in Sol's light, giving Saturn a truly royal air.

The etheric information we have accessed names lead as the metal of Saturn. This is a curious irony, for Saturn's chemical composition makes it the lightest of this system's planets. However, our sensors indicate that the planet's core may be quite dense, and this would make for a more understandable association with the heavy element.

The elegant, highly organized rings are symbolic of structure and form—the foundations of things upon which further growth is determined. This capacity to organize also speaks of clarity and farsightedness—talents at the heart of advice, wise counsel, and proper planning. Taken to extremes, however, this orderly aspect could invoke excessive discipline and inflexibility.

Our scans are also quick to recognize that those who exhibit the showy brilliance of Saturn can easily be blinded by their own beauty, becoming overly self-confident, cold, and removed from others. With appropriate balance, however, Saturn symbolizes an all-encompassing, radiant influence that surrounds a highly evolved consciousness that is sensitive on the outside and solid at the core.

Drawing the outstanding symbol of the Saturn card motivates us to get our affairs in order. It advises us to make certain that all important considerations are clearly laid out and that everyone involved knows where they stand and what they're expected to do.

This does not mean analyzing everything to death, but rather having a distinct vision of how things must come together. Our guiding image will then act as a template wherein all factors and diverse talents can automatically fall into place with minimal thought or supervision.

It is suggested that we both give and pay attention to ideas and advice that could help solidify the big picture. In the process, however, we need to be careful to avoid attempts to take the power of others or give our power away.

The Saturn card shows us that we are surrounded by all that we require and that we may need to search within the different layers of our being to become aware of the abilities we innately contain. Though it is good to be recognized for our gifts, we must also be mindful that it does not always serve us to be the center of attention. Natural charm and beauty are more often enhanced by graceful humility and a genuine desire to be of service.

Summoning Saturn also means it is time to assess the basic structure of our lives. Do our relationships, our jobs, and our living spaces really offer us the opportunities that encourage creativity, growth, and new challenges? Are we living up to our soul's true purpose by being fully who we are? Drawing the Saturn card may mean it is time for a philosophical examination of our lives and being bold enough to make the changes we know will allow us to live our deepest truths.

PLANETS

CHIRON

SOL 8:
CHIRON

Log of the survey ship Wanderer.
Excerpt from the survey of the Sol star system:

Sol 8, which the Earth's inhabitants have only recently named Chiron, is a small, asteroidlike minor planet between Saturn and Uranus, two gas giants.

Like the asteroid belt, Chiron symbolizes a type of threshold to be crossed—a bridge linking the physical energy of Saturn with the metaphysical qualities of Uranus. It acts as a sort of transitional gate, a fulcrum of balance between the paradoxical qualities of the inner and outer worlds.

Our sensors indicate that Chiron may have found its present orbit after being dislodged from its residence in this system's outer band of asteroids called Oort's Cloud. If so, then Chiron represents a very new energy as far as the planets go and might signal that the Sol system is going through an important transition at present.

Chiron and the outer planets beyond Saturn were unknown to the ancient inhabitants of Earth. No metallic associations were made for them when they were discovered since that practice ended some time ago.

However, Chiron follows Saturn in sequence and represents transition. The metal of Saturn is lead and the first transitional element following lead in the periodic table of elements is called actinium. This might mean that some action is required to smoothly facilitate whatever transition is in progress.

Chiron's tiny form, perched between two such enormous worlds, make it the symbolic "eye of the needle." This means its energy compresses and focuses events, allowing passage to the next level only when all clutter has been stripped away.

Our psychotronic projector has ascertained that Chiron is the archetypal reflection of the transformational cycle now dominant within this system as characterized by the spiritual awakening of the inhabitants of Sol 3. This is, therefore, a time of great potential and promise, but we do not envy them the physical, emotional, mental, and spiritual lessons they will learn during this shift. That this will be a "character building" experience is an understatement.

We have observed a curious synchronicity in that Chiron has the same fifty-year orbit around Sol that the white dwarf star Sirius B, called Digitaria by some Earth inhabitants, has around its primary star, Sirius. This similarity of vibrational and size relationship signals that Chiron, like Sirius B, represents the inner eye that opens the mind, initiating it to a higher level of conscious awareness and choice.

In receiving the Chiron card, we are shown the way from problem to solution by viewing the circumstances as opportunity rather than impediment.

Though a small, or minor, planet, Chiron's energy is extremely potent. Like a homeopathic remedy, a small dose of Chiron's vibration can initiate widespread healing. As the symbol of transition, Chiron points out that just the right pressure applied at the precise spot can cause massive transformation in our state of being and, subsequently, the quality of our experiences. In other words, less is sometimes more.

As with all shifts, we cannot change merely a portion of ourselves; we must make the journey as whole beings. Thus, Chiron calls us to open ourselves to our deepest pain—our wounded selves—in order to undertake a thorough self-assessment, integrate what we need, and leave behind whatever beliefs and behavior patterns are not conducive to where we are headed. The "extra baggage" cannot fit into our new paradigm. In Earth's ancient mythology, Chiron was a centaur who was known as the "Wounded Healer."

This is a time for refinement—an ascension from the lower energies to the higher. This is like the alchemist's symbolic transmutation of lead into gold, which, though perhaps a literal pursuit, chiefly represented the growth of spirit from a base to a more evolved vibration of light. It may be time to transition from simply being students and realize that we have gifts of experience and wisdom to share and teach.

Last, but far from least, Chiron means "hand." The element actinium, which we have associated with Chiron, is similar to the word "action." This seems an appropriate correlation considering that our hands are what we take action with. Thus it "rules" all created works, including the Contact Cards themselves!

If Chiron has been conjured at this time, then a deeper meaning can be gleaned from each symbol represented by the spread of the cards and choices can be made for great and lasting change in our lives. A suggestion would be to use Chiron as the first card of a new full-spiral spread to see how that change might manifest.

SOL 9:
URANUS

Log of the survey ship Wanderer.
Excerpt from the survey of the Sol star system:

The first world beyond the transitional bridge of Chiron is exactly what one would expect to find: a planet of unexpected strangeness.

First of all, the axis of Uranus is radically tipped toward Sol, creating not north and south poles, but east and west poles instead. In addition, like Venus, Uranus rotates on its axis in the opposite direction from most planets in this system. Because of its distance from Sol and its eccentric inclination, each Uranian hemisphere spends more than four decades in darkness before spending the next four receiving Sol's light.

We scan that the depths of this world border on the chaos of the unconscious mind. It is associated with energetic, insightful, and even scientific breakthrough that accelerates progress.

However, in an unstable environment, these propensities of individuality and nonconformity can lead to wild and unpredictable circumstances of insane proportions. Within the realm of Uranus's rule there is either genius or madness, shamans or shams.

While surveying Uranus, our craft experienced sudden short circuits and surges of electrical energy. We attribute this to feedback in our psychically sensitive scanners—a sure sign of Uranus's connection with metaphysical matters.

This is a world of sweeping and revolutionary change.

Tapping its titanic energy opens surprising channels of information that once allowed to flow may be impossible to turn off. The extreme conditions of light and dark that mark Uranus's orbit symbolize the fine line between insight and evolution or anarchy and annihilation.

When Uranus deigns to pay a visit, we should expect the unexpected. Upheavals in social consciousness and increased sensitivity to previously hidden undercurrents of change mark the energy of this card.

This is a highly charged, psychic symbol that taps into the chaos that precedes all creation—that bubbling caldron of potentiality from which we sample our sensate realities.

Uranian energy moves in a contrary way, opposite to the general flow of society and what it often holds to be common sense. This is the energy that sees beyond the normal. Its elemental namesake, uranium, is able to radiate energy that penetrates most barriers. Similarly, Uranus penetrates the veils surrounding secrets and allows us to peer into larger realms and access higher knowledge.

Just as each half of Uranus spends forty years in darkness and then forty years in light, this card symbolizes the average forty-year cycle of human transformation that culminates in what is often called "mid-life crisis." However, this transition does not need to be experienced as a crisis. Drawing this card can inspire us to embrace the changes in our lives with eager vitality as we come out of the darkness or confusion of our youth and enter a cycle of clarity and wisdom.

SOL 10:
NEPTUNE

Log of the survey ship Wanderer.
Excerpt from the survey of the Sol star system:

In appearance, Sol 10, called Neptune, is very similar to Sol 9, Uranus. They are about the same size and coloration, being bluish-green, although Neptune's axis is of relatively normal, north-south inclination.

Neptune's orbit is almost perfectly circular, which aligns well with its water symbolism in that a drop of water forms a perfect sphere in the gravity-free void of deep space. Our scanners take this water analogy further, extending Neptune's harmonic to all things liquid, including music and movement that flows in natural rhythms.

Currents, whether in the sea or in the air, are within the auspices of Neptune and determine the direction and, thus, the outcome of all endeavors immersed in its vibration. Just as schools of fish live in the ocean or flocks of birds traverse the skies, so does Neptune guide groups in their quests.

And as water has many different states of being, Neptune symbolizes imagination, emotion, and illusion, each respectively representing distinct, transitional, and ethereal qualities of perception.

The shadow side of Neptune is like a stagnant pond. The penchant for group conformity can quickly suppress all individual ability and initiative, thus sacrificing self-empowerment.

We have decided to move on before our survey ship's

agenda is clouded by Neptune's influential pull and our crew drowns in a sea of dreams.

If Neptune is flowing in our direction, it is advantageous to get in touch with our imagination and sense of timing. It is important to become keenly aware of the direction in which we are being pulled by the currents of the events in our lives.

This card calls for us to become more fluid—to navigate around the obstacles by adopting a more giving or yielding nature. This does not mean that we yield to those things we know do not represent our truth, but rather that we soften our approach to life and our interactions within it. We can shift our attitude to be more harmonious and melodious in our discourses with ourselves and others—to swim in a sea of love.

To swim, we must keep moving, and Neptune's shadow warns that if we do not continue to flow through dynamic action, we might sink to the bottom. Care must be taken lest we drown in some idyllic illusion that all things will take care of themselves without us and so let our responsibilities float off and our lives evaporate.

The true power of this card lies in the sense of freedom that comes with inner peace. In this state, all joyful actions are effortless and we find ourselves surrounded by buoyant, supportive, and limitless energy.

If we have dipped into Neptune's waters, we may also have already gone through a recent transition and become our more spiritual selves. If so, we may need to take time to adjust to our new level of ethereal vibration and choose how to apply this energy to our more dense physical surroundings. This can be confusing at first, but if we continue to trust our natural flow, we will always wind up exactly where we belong.

PLANETS

PLUTO?

SOL II:
PLUTO

Log of the survey ship Wanderer.
Excerpt from the survey of the Sol star system:

Our ship is now approximately four billion Earth miles from Sol. Very little of the sun's light reaches this desolate little planet.

Though ostensibly a gaseous world, Pluto is so cold that all the gas has condensed into a rock-hard shell around the planet's small core. It is like the dead husk of a world, and it was certainly a surprise when our etheric sensors picked up Pluto's role as this system's archetypal lord of the underworld.

Because its atmosphere is frozen in perpetual suspension, Pluto also represents hidden secrets—knowledge that is hard to access. Everything we could know about this world is buried in its mantle of ice, and so Pluto is also connected to all things that are buried, meaning not only the dead but treasures as well.

Pluto makes our scanners work very hard to extract what meager information we can. This tells us that the very act of searching for knowledge is also associated with Pluto's clandestine quality.

Pluto's large moon, Charon, has been named for the archetypal Earth being who assists others in crossing from the land of the living to the land of the dead. Its close position to Pluto and its similar size imply that Pluto's energy is always accompanied by assistance and guidance while making the transition from old life to new life or while

investigating clues or attempting to access occult knowledge or secrets. However, a negative frequency within this
search could lead to obsession or the assumption that there
is a "life and death" need to accomplish a specific goal.

Plutonium is the element of this world. It is utilized in
the making of atomic bombs and creates deadly radioactive
fallout when exploded. Therefore we are cautioned to exercise infinite patience in all things we undertake under
Pluto's influence so our work remains vital and uncontami-
nated.

On the positive side, we know that death is never the
end, but rather only the beginning of a new cycle. Life goes
on, and for now, so must our ship.

The energy of Pluto is not easily discernible since its
very nature deals with issues that remain hidden. However,
if we have been allowed a glimpse of this card, we are being
invited to seek out that clandestine knowledge so that we
may more fully know ourselves or what is occurring invisi-
bly all around us.

As symbolized by Pluto's moon, Charon, we may be
required to make a crossing from day into metaphorical
night in order to discover such cloaked intelligence, for
some things can be perceived only with "night vision." In
doing so, we must be alert to every subtle sound and clue,
seeing things in a different way than before and learning to
understand how they may be connected along invisible
lines.

On such a journey, our inner lights must be bright.
Otherwise, we can all too easily fall prey to obsessive paranoia and excessive fear of shadows that contain important
signposts and unrecognized guidance.

In walking this path, we must be steadfast and vigilant within our intentions and integrity so as not to be seduced by the darkness within our souls. If we acknowledge Pluto's ability to balance and ground our lighter selves, we can become powerful seers and inspired magicians of manifestation.

Without that balance, this planet can lure us into lunatic fugues or sorcery by stealth. We could become the ultimate prisoner, trapped in a maze of mindless, self-destructive machinations that will fill our lives with untold misfortune.

By the vibration of this card, all things can be brought from the dark into the light so that spiritual truths can be revealed. Drawing Pluto invites us on a journey into our innermost selves, so our souls can retrieve those aspects left too long in the darkness.

SOL 12:
NIBIRU

Log of the survey ship Wanderer.
Excerpt from the survey of the Sol star system:

Neither our physical sensors nor our psychotronic scanners can glean much from this mysterious outer world except a faint echo of a name: Nibiru.

Nibiru's orbit seems quite elliptical. At one time long ago, it may have been much closer to Sol and may have been capable of supporting life—perhaps not indigenous life, but at least a temporary base as indicated by our sensors.

We wonder if that archaic race, whoever they might have been, had any contact with or influence upon the early inhabitants of Earth. If so, it might explain some of the unusual cultural attributes we recorded while scanning that ocean planet.

If the ancient Earth legends about an extraterrestrial race called the Anunnaki are true, those beings may have been the creator gods responsible for initiating the human species. Since Nibiru is so far out in its orbit at present, it is difficult for our scanners to retrieve any but the strongest memories of those remote events.

Our long-range scanners detect no other planetary bodies on the periphery of this system. With nothing else to explore, we will leave Nibiru behind—an enigmatic monument standing eternal guard in the empty night of space.

Nibiru is the Contact Card that deals with pure mystery and the challenge of the unknown. This energy impels us to solve the riddle of who we really are and why we have joined in this passion play of physical reality. It instructs us to get back to basics and get in touch with our most fundamental qualities so that we may build our lives on solid foundations.

This card pushes us to take that great leap of faith into what at first may appear as a dark void. However, upon landing on the other side it becomes a supportive womb full of new perspectives and possibilities.

Nibiru encourages us to remain neutral at the beginning of any experience—to not automatically and unconsciously assign either positive or negative meaning, but to make a clear, discerning choice that all events contain limitless possibilities. Nibiru assures us that the meanings we give to our situations completely determine the effects we experience in return.

Many times we may wish to impose familiar meanings on new surroundings, but by doing so we rob ourselves of rich realities that could be more than we are capable of imagining. We are asked to remember that the beginning of wisdom is to know that we don't know.

CROP CIRCLES

CARD	ATTRIBUTE
Barbury Castle	Body/Mind/Spirit
Crucifix	Stop
Earth Goddess	Goddess/Female
Flower of Life	Beginnings
Galactic	Insight/Resources
Hermaphrodite	Harmony
Lightning Strike	Power
Mandlebrot	Foundation
Mr. Curlyman	Trust
Sun God	God/Male
Swastika	Journey
The Key	Treasures

CROP CIRCLES

Though many people are still either unfamiliar with crop circles ("agriglyphs") or debate their authenticity, they are such an otherworldly phenomenon it seemed appropriate to include them in Contact Cards.

With their mathematical precision and beauty, crop circles are certainly a message of some kind. It is commonly believed (but not proven) that they are extraterrestrially created. Whatever their origins, they possess higher-dimensional qualities that force us to look beyond the boundaries of our everyday worldview in seeking an answer to their purpose.

All the crop circles depicted here are authentic in name and configuration. They were each chosen specifically for the symbolic energy given to them at the time of their discovery.

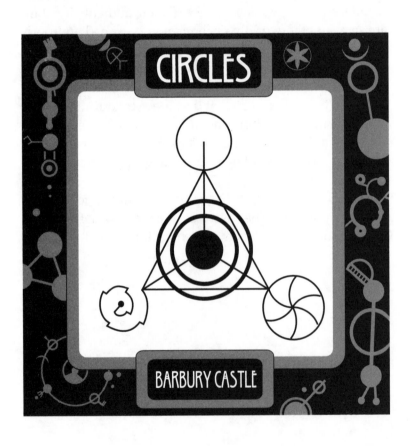

CIRCLES

BARBURY CASTLE

BARBURY CASTLE

If you stand upon a single foot, will you not tire and topple to the ground?

If you stride from left to right, will you not eventually need to rest from your balancing act? What, then will hold you upright? Two points make only a single line, which offers little support.

Three firm footings are required to provide true stability. This is the balance of beginning, middle, and end— the ménage à trois of body, mind, and spirit.

I am the trinary archetype of the inner and outer realities that imperceptibly combine to form the threshold of personal identity.

I am the tetrahedral prism of consciousness that transforms the holographic light of knowingness into the spectrum of beliefs, emotions, and thoughts that pattern life's experiences.

I am the trinity of heaven, hell, and purgatory—those eternal attributes that drive the engines in all pursuits of pleasure, pain, and apathy.

My apex is the fulcrum under the balance beam—the twilight between day and night.

My triune form is the scaffolding that frames the heroic myths of antiquity. I weave tales that wind from unexpected discovery through perilous journey and culminate in thoughtful resolution.

My symbol is the mark of alchemy: the transmutation of the primal into the sublime.

I am the magician that embodies earth, sea, and sky—

the glyph of evolution that inspires each being to know itself, and the world, as a marriage of matter and light.

A child is born to explore the possibilities of life. An adolescent combines the panoply of choices to suit itself. An adult reaps the fruit of the chosen path and learns that while the first attempt may be fraught with assumptions and the second leap can be frightening, for those with insight, wisdom, and experience, the third time's often the charm.

The archetypal energy of Barbury Castle embodies the balance of body, mind, and spirit. With this card, we can explore the three essential ingredients that comprise our personalities—beliefs, emotions, and behavior—to be certain all are operating with clarity and harmony.

The aptly named castle symbolizes the house that is our physical being. The integrity of the structure of our lives relies on the accuracy of the blueprint (beliefs), the energy of the builders (emotions), and the quality of the building materials (behavior). If any or all of these are substandard, our houses, which are ourselves and our lives, will be weak and vulnerable to natural turbulences.

This card, therefore, represents process. It is here that we get in touch with our inner journey—where we have come from, where we are, and where we are going—and make the adjustments or clarifications in our bodies, minds, and spirits that will bring about a stronger sense of balance in ourselves and our service to others.

Above all, Barbury Castle assures us that if we combine a strong willingness to grow and learn with continuous forward motion, we will encounter all the information necessary to understand the meaning and purpose of our lives. We must not give up . . . perseverance brings experience that leads to wisdom.

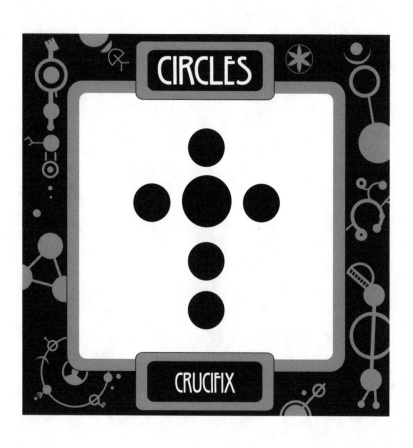

CIRCLES

CRUCIFIX

CRUCIFIX

If I am planted in your path, take heed! I am the warning sign, the guardian with flaming sword, the crossed bones beneath the leering skull. Go back! Turn around! Retrace the steps that have led to my presence in your life.

Time is suspended and life hangs in the balance when my arms unfold. I am the emissary of fortune and fate. My mantle of office calls all decisions into question for reevaluation.

I am the blade's edge, used to cut the ties that bind. I am the crosshairs that enforce a penetrating focus of intent and shatter the cage of expectation and repetition.

I am death and resurrection. I am the moment when the comforting cloak of habitual attachment is cast off like a snake's skin to reveal the glistening core of simple truth.

I stand firm, vigilant in my duty to deflect the blind, headlong rush toward doom and defeat. I am the last outpost of sanity and salvation, perched on the border of the scorching sands of denial.

I reassure all who encounter my shadow that the way back does not need to be long, for the path of least resistance is the path of the true self. Though the new road may be winding, it will be the most rewarding, for the shortest distance between two points is not always a straight line.

I am the symbol of surrender and serenity. The spirit is released in the sigh and is carried to freedom on the wings of willingness. Let go!

Resistance to the self is the harbinger of all disease, and fear of change is its symptom. If the light of clarity is allowed to shine, the shadows that once seemed solid will quickly fade away.

If the Crucifix has crossed our path, we must pay serious attention to where we are headed. Continuing on our present path may lead to an unfortunate outcome, and we must not be swayed by our ego's impatience to bulldoze our way through to some desired goal.

Very often, we may assume that the path that takes the least amount of time is the best and most efficient one. However, a vehicle that doesn't take time to pull off the road for fuel may run out before arriving at its destination, making the trip take much longer than if the necessary detour had been taken. The winding path allows us to gather what we need in order to more fully appreciate and enjoy the trip as well as the destination.

While it is good to have a goal to pull us along the path, we must surrender the assumption that it's the only goal on the map. Quite often, taking the unexpected route can bring us to a place more beautiful than what we initially set out to find.

This card strongly advises that we pause a moment to look back along the road we have traveled. It encourages us to go back to whatever crossroads there may have been and choose the path most representative of our nature and our joy rather than the one we were expected to take.

On the shadow side, the Crucifix is a sign that guilt, or the attempt to take responsibility for the actions of others, may be the strongest motivating force underlying our actions and that it's time to clear this out of our energy. Balance and creative compromise can be employed in our relationships and endeavors, but sacrifice and martyrdom will only nail us to our unresolved pain and ingrained feelings of worthlessness.

CIRCLES

EARTH GODDESS

EARTH GODDESS

I am the Earth mother, Gaia—the cradle of life, the womb of creation.

My breath is the warm, tropical breeze that lovingly caresses the deep green forest ferns. My perfume is the flower's fragrance on a rain-washed spring day.

I am open, yielding, inviting. I receive the life-giving waters that seep into my fertile soil so my seeds can germinate and fill my fields with sweet grasses.

My symbol is as patient as the pyramids, supportive as the stones, accepting as the sky. It is my nature to nurture; my love is unconditional.

Some believe that my gentility makes me weak, but my power is in subtlety and persistence, like the small mountain stream that after aeons carves a mile-deep canyon through solid rock.

I am the medicine woman—the healer who knows the magic potency of herbs and can speak the language of the trees.

I am the mystery of the night and the cycles of the Moon—the Babylonian harlot, the chaste priestess, and the the sanctified Magdalene. I peer into watery depths, calling forth visions of Delphic proportions, and my songs are incantations that beget life from nothingness.

To bear my mark is to know the birth pangs that accompany all new endeavors. Intuition and insight are my farseeing eyes. The radiant heart is the soul mate of the burning intellect. The freedom to feel allows all children, be they flesh or idea, to mature into knowing adults.

I am mother and daughter, sister and lover. I embody the unbridled joy and serenity of the eternal Goddess.

The Earth Goddess bids that we strengthen our connection to our feminine qualities and our ties to nature.

This card signals a time for soft silence—a time to hush the constant inner mental dialogue that often accompanies our hectic lives. It counsels us to relax within our quiet centers, as a flower folds its petals in at night. If we allow ourselves that nurturing space, we can heal our deepest pains and emerge with the stunning radiance of a summer bloom.

The Earth Goddess also instructs that the expression of great power does not require great force. Slow, steady, and persistent application of intention will often accomplish a lot more. With the support of the Earth Goddess, all our endeavors can come from the heart, and the desires we birth into manifestation can have long, happy, and healthy lives.

Should we be in the midst of a particularly painful or difficult transition when we get this card, we can rely on the goddess within ourselves to guide us by drawing our attention to those attitudes, opportunities, and actions that would contain the greatest expressions of unconditional love.

CIRCLES

FLOWER OF LIFE

FLOWER OF LIFE

I am the very essence of dreams—the wellspring of new possibilities, the beginning of life in all its forms. I underlie the fabric of reality as its blueprint, its template, its genetic helix.

The physical universe relies upon me for substance and transubstantiation. I am the crucible and the forge that give birth to new existences.

I am the nurturing womb that supports reality as it is. Yet I also impart the driving urgency for change that allows that reality to become all that it can be. To flow within the radiant dream of my ever-expanding waves of transformation is to be open to growth on all levels of being.

To blend within my harmonic tones is to unconditionally respect all aspects of personal vibration—to cherish each individuated facet separately and to love them all together as an integrated whole. I am the weaver who spins each delicate strand of life into a richly complex tapestry of shape and spirit.

If gifted with my symbol, any new endeavor will ripple outward like waves in a pond, filling the world with myriad reflections of creativity. My languid spiral is an invitation to open in innocent vulnerability to my loving, universal warmth and blossom like a fresh flower, its petals reaching like wide-open arms in total acceptance of the uniqueness of its soul.

I am all generations contained within a single seed. I am the pure potential of inception and renewal. I am the eternal promise of spring.

The Flower of Life is one of the strongest symbols of success, especially for new paths, endeavors, and relationships.

This card reveals that all the ingredients are present to best allow current circumstances to come to abundant fruition with very little outside help. In other words, the situation is exactly what we need to receive the greatest reflection of our true selves. The challenge is to remain trusting and not attempt to force the details in the way our ego-based fears might want us to.

The light of our faith, the water of our joy, and the soil of our positive intentions will automatically bring about a rich, colorful garden filled with the delicate fragrances of every imaginable flower our consciousnesses can grow. Our lives can be filled with diverse treasures and expanding ecstasy.

The Flower of Life card warns us not to poison our innocent nature with doubts about our deservability and worth. If it were true that our deepest and most loving wishes for a happy life were incapable of being fulfilled or that we really didn't deserve them, they would not reside at the very hearts of our beings. Happiness, joy, love, and abundance are not mere goals—they are the essence of our souls.

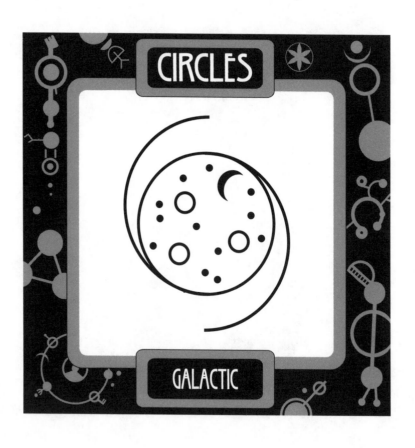

CIRCLES

GALACTIC

GALACTIC

I know that all truths are true and all perspectives valid for those who live by their edicts. I take and amalgamate from the palette of views what best defines my singular being. Leaving nothing out, I am free to choose from all possible realities—to taste and savor the incomparable array of life's subtle and sublime textures or to partake of more pungent and intoxicating fare.

By this device do I expand into a maelstrom of meaningful self-discoveries. I peer through crystal-clear windows of opportunity upon parallel paths that stretch ever outward, each path connecting with multiple avenues of opportunity.

I am the all-encompassing passion for life and discovery that inspires adventurers to search far and wide for the tantalizing and elusive experiences that form the rich soil of their soul's growth.

I am the sharing of stories around the fires that stave off the darkness. I am the gathering of the clans. I am the countless generations of explorers breaking through into the walled chambers of entombed history and knowledge.

Nothing is wasted in my regime. Just as forests wither in winter to form the loam for the buds of spring, so do I till and plow old ideas, sifting through the compost, searching for the new green shoots of fresh revelations.

With glacial patience and relentless persistence, I scour the surface of consciousness for clues that might lead to deeper truths to slake my unending appetite for pristine horizons.

The Galactic is the all-encompassing symbol that reminds us to use our resources to their best advantage. It exhorts us to fully utilize our personal talents and the rich opportunities in every situation and extend them out to impact our world at large.

As our galaxy rotates, we are carried through cycle after cycle. We learn to use, reinvent, and reuse every tool at our disposal so that nothing is squandered or taken for granted.

However, lurking within the Galactic's shadow is the shriveled heart of the miser, that penchant to hoard and use the same things in the same ways over and over again until they become useless and worn out. Even when we seek to extract every drop from what we have, there must always be some fresh ingredient or new perspective added if the old substance is to be transformed into an instrument of contemporary use.

The Galactic card teaches us to recycle all our resources to maximum benefit while being simultaneously open to receiving new sources of energy and information. We can then incorporate them into our established methods in ways that cause us to adapt and grow rather than to repeat and stagnate.

CIRCLES

HERMAPHRODITE

HERMAPHRODITE

I dance with myself. I am my own perfect soul mate—a marriage of opposites, a dichotomous dream.

I am yin and yang, night and day, female and male in harmonious accord. My symbol is the essence of balance—a partnership of polarities that melds into perfect empathetic union.

I see all sides of every issue and gauge all possible outcomes, insuring that each step will proceed from the center of my being. In vulnerability, I find strength; in obstacles, I create opportunities; in doubt, I discover the seeds of certainty.

Paradox is my power. Should I confess to a lack of confidence, I am confident about my lack. Should I succumb to a lack of faith, then that is an unshakable belief. To accept the depths is to acknowledge the heights. Thus do I at once create and cancel my own opposing forces.

I am the reflection of completion, yet simultaneously the magnetic attractor of unfinished symphonies crying out for resolution.

I am self-generating, self-motivating, and self-perpetuating—my own inspiration, catalyst, and manifestor. I am the twin flame, the mirror image, and the window to my own soul.

To accept my symbol is to accept all antitheses with an egalitarian air. It is to know that all choices are equal until arbitrarily assigned meanings tip the balance toward a biased interpretation.

Once the dark and the light are integrated, there exists

no resistance. Thus, no power can stave off the outcome that best serves the good of all.

The Hermaphrodite card is an invitation to embrace the totality of our being and all the dichotomy or polarity that we contain.

This energy teaches us to remain neutral within all situations and to not impose our outdated meanings and labels upon them. Instead, we can learn to accept ourselves for who and what we are, finding strength in the blending and balancing of all our aspects. Rather than assuming that certain qualities don't belong within us, we can rely on them to give us a unique inner perspective and act as a foundational support or stepping stone for the attributes we prefer to exhibit outwardly.

By utilizing the Hermaphrodite's awareness, we can also be more sensitive to the feelings and choices of others who may seem different from us. They are only revealing an aspect that we ourselves contain but have chosen not to express as prominently.

This card bears testimony to the power of paradox as a teaching tool. When we find ourselves assuming that only our viewpoint is valid, we need to remember that we also must contain its opposite, since nothing can exist with only one side.

Drawing the Hermaphrodite indicates that we may be facing a difficult situation or decision. If we spend some time viewing the circumstance from the other perspectives involved, new solutions may present themselves. No person is an island; all interactions and relationships reflect yet another aspect or attribute we ourselves contain.

CIRCLES

LIGHTNING STRIKE

LIGHTNING STRIKE

I come crashing through all barriers with great power. Nothing stands in my way. I bridge heaven and Earth and unite all polarities through the center of my being.

Swift and strong, I strike without hesitation, bringing instant illumination where darkness once reigned.

When I speak, forests fall silent in the wake of my rumbling voice, which resounds in all corners of Earth and sky.

Only kindred spirits of high energy can be in my company, for I burn away all deception, revealing the naked core of truth and light. My path demands great commitment and focus—a knowledge of what must be done and the boldness to take immediate action.

Reflect upon my form as the mark of courage, for if you heed my call, you must be prepared to announce your arrival and your intention to the world. You are capable of shining with the brilliance of the Sun and igniting change in all that you touch.

If you choose my symbol, I will teach you the way of the elemental fire that is the very passion of life itself.

Walk with me and live in the now, in fearless command of the gifts bestowed upon you by creation's flame; accept your legacy among the fires of heaven. Dispel the shadows where demons cower, and become the shining path that lights the way for others to follow.

Lightning Strike is a card of great power and illumination. This symbol shouts for us to get moving on anything we are hesitant about—to jump in and forge ahead with bold assurance and conviction, and to do it now!

This card is about passion and creation. Within this energy, there is no time for dour or dull dispositions, only activity and expression.

However, even lightning can cast a shadow. Unless guided along appropriate channels, this energy can be overzealous, charring everything it touches that is not insulated from its undiminished voltage. With sensitivity and compassionate focus, we can allow this energy to flow along the lines that empower us and everyone with whom we come in contact.

With the level of power this card commands, it is critical that we remember to remain firmly grounded so we will not burn ourselves out. Our attention on what we are doing and our intention as to why we are on this course must be aligned and clearly understood so that the rapid change that follows our actions will spread out in beneficial ways to all within our range of impact.

Attracting the Lightning Strike card may indicate that we are on the verge of a powerful spiritual illumination. When we become excited by the possibility of a new world opening before us, we can remember that our ability to access spirit is directly proportional to the degree that we remain grounded in the here and now.

MANDELBROT

I, that is, the proper noun, meaning me, am precisely where I belong, that is, location, meaning here and now.

I could not be other than I am nor elsewhere or elsewhen. I am absolutely, completely, and perfectly in the right place at the right time doing exactly what I ought to be doing.

I am the foundation of my own structure—the seed of my flower and the rungs of the ladder up which I climb. I am both the secret and the revelation, the blueprint and the building, the thread and the tapestry.

I am the prime ingredient of all things; without me, only chaos would reign. From an infinitesimal point to multitudinous dimensionality, I define the proportions that each will take and see to it that my laws are kept.

There are those who assume that my parameters must be broken in order to birth miracles. What nonsense! Miracles blossom where I am fully understood, spiraling inward and outward simultaneously.

There are those who protest that I am rigid and rote, the symbol without a soul. Yet in a fraction of a second, I can be infinitely transcendent.

Though in truth (which is relative) I may be fathomless to many, I am always accountable for my actions. For those who are equal to the task, I am easy as π.

The Mandelbrot card reflects the need for precision within our actions and clarity within each choice that we make.

This is a foundational energy. If great care is not taken to make sure that all important factors are in their proper places, total chaos will result.

Big things are built upon small things. Attention to detail is critical within this energy. We must not act rashly or haphazardly. The slightest deviation from the purity of our path will generate mutations in all subsequent avenues, and it will soon be evident that we have an uncontrollable monster on our hands.

The Mandelbrot points out that cause and effect, initiation and outcome, and the means and the end are all one concept. There is no process by which we can learn to live life except in the living of it.

This card is also a strong symbol of synchronicity, where we can take note that the so-called coincidences in our lives are not really random accidents, but the logical orchestrations of our choices. Free will sets up our destinies, and it is our destiny to exercise our free will. We are the creators of our self-fulfilling prophecies.

We create all the realities we experience, and in manifesting the Mandelbrot, we can expand into the realization that our underlying belief equations will always generate only the reality that fits the template we have created. Each time we change any variable within the formula of our definitions of life, we immediately alter the outcome across the board.

However, just as the Mandelbrot curves back upon itself, each fractal part being identical no matter how large or small, we are reminded that we cannot base the changes within us on whether the exterior reality has changed or not. We must respond differently to the reality, even if it appears the same as before, in order to know we are truly different. Once we have mastered that positive attitude, the exterior world is then free to conform to our balanced and peaceful selves.

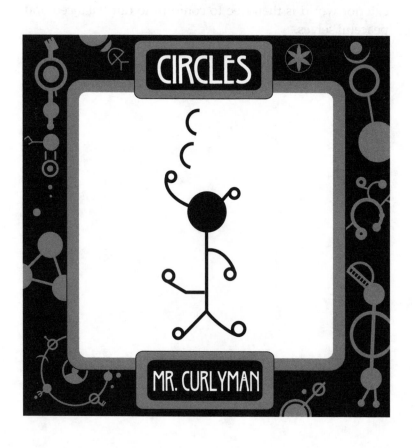

MR. CURLYMAN

Catch me if you can, though I am fickle as the wind.

I curve and swerve, darting to and fro, abandoning all conventions society imposes upon those of timid temperament. Though I may appear reckless and foolhardy to more somber dispositions, I am guided by unseen hands that stay me from the pitfalls on my path.

I am as ethereal as a shadow, yet my laughter has the power to heal even the sick at heart. I am a will-o'-the-wisp, flitting through bright blue skies laced with perennial rainbows, yet I am the secret of everlasting peace that strengthens the soul.

Come play with me in the castles of imagination where everything is possible. Depression is vanquished in the shine of my smile. Sadness is dissolved in the glint of my eyes. Apathy melts in the infectious warmth of my carefree spirit.

My symbol shouts "freedom!" from the mountaintops. I am the patron saint of all iconoclasts, the muse of all artists, the heart of every child.

I am the trickster who plays the idiot—a mere clown to uninspired minds, but a mirror of mystery to undaunted explorers of the Infinite. It's a cosmic joke to take life too seriously, for the first step toward true enlightenment is to lighten up.

The counterparts of Mr. Curlyman are the Fool in the traditional tarot and the Coyote Trickster in Native American lore.

This energy is elusive to all but those who are willing to play, to be children at heart. In this way we are open to discovering the deepest secrets of creation.

Mr. Curlyman asks us to come out of our shells and run through the flowering fields with abandon. He calls to us to drop our facades of civilization, our thin veneers of approved behavior, and shed society's conventions in favor of the freedom to be ourselves.

This does not mean that we tumble headfirst over the nearest precipice, thinking that we have no need to be alert to our surroundings. Instead, when we awaken from our civilized slumber, we see with clearer sight than ever before and know that every footfall is guided by our higher selves. In this way, we will never falter as we move through life as freely as the wind.

Imagination combined with intuitive play can allow us to reclaim our initial innocence, even as we mature into beings of profound and gentle wisdom. A child does not know that it also teaches as it learns because it is lost in the enjoyment of the moment.

CIRCLES

SUN GOD

SUN G☉D

Resplendent and glorious am I, the Sun God, who casts beneficent rays of light and life and dispels the shadows of the night.

I inspire new growth and am the driving engine for the changing seasons. I assert my aureate presence through every window that is opened to greet the dawn.

Rise and shine! Action is the order of the day. I am Helios, whose fiery chariot leads the way. My incandescence illuminates the farthest horizons and reveals each rise, fall, and bend of the journey's path.

My radiant luster is for all but those who deign to reside in darkness. Seekers of light are my children, and I am their eternal father.

Lest it appear that my symbol is too forward, my energy also urges wisdom, sagacity, and the honing of shimmering intellect. I am the judge, the arbiter of justice—the sword of reason and the slayer of doubt.

I am the wizard—the high priest of alchemical transformation. I am the silver lining adorning every cloud.

I am the father and the son, the brother and the lover. I am the majesty and the miracle of intention, conviction, and regeneration—the strong, steady hand of the eternal God.

With the Sun God card, we are assured of our ability to walk assertively down our path, firm in our faith that as long as we remain humble and are open to learn, we will always be shown the correct and most effortless route.

We are protected as well as guided by this energy. If we are clear that our convictions are truly representative of our inner knowing and are not simply our ego's apprehensions, then all outcomes will favor us, no matter that others may have negative intentions toward us. As expounded within spiritual literature, we can "walk through the valley of death" and honestly "fear no evil" as long as our hearts and minds shine with a radiance that reflects the light of the Infinite.

This card also illuminates the danger of allowing our ego to assume that it is in charge of our total being. When doing its designated job of helping us to focus our consciousness through the mask of personality, the ego is a good tool. But if the ego is allowed to replace our higher, knowing self, it will attempt to control every detail of our lives instead of granting equal time to intuition. If care is not taken, this tendency can quickly inflate into megalomania.

When we are fair and generous, we will always remain the champions of justice and not merely the arbiters of law and order.

CIRCLES

SWASTIKA

SWASTIKA

I am the ancient one, the oldest of symbols, for I am the wheel of life. Choices radiate from my hub—the countless paths of experience and its attendant lessons.

I am the crossroads of decision and the arbiter of karmic consequence, for the harvest can come only from what has been sown. The circle cannot exist without its center; only from there can creation manifest.

Yet even as the circle is perceived as the experience, this is only illusion. Goals are not something to be achieved nor is process a means to an end, for the journey and the goal are one.

I am the reminder that every encounter is part of the path. If defined as such, the knowledge gained will help consciousness to expand. But if circumstances are feared, then my wheel will spin only doubt and confusion, for I am a mirror of intention: I can reflect only the truth.

I am the symbol of the sorcerer's path, the shaman's journey. Wisdom and transformation are the rewards of remaining true to the self.

My arms are strong and supportive and always spin toward the light. To flow against my current is allowed, but this will always conjure dark storms deep within the soul that must someday be vanquished by the heat of the sun.

I am the migration from innocence through mystery and finally to enlightenment. I am the dance between free will and destiny.

To live each day to the fullest is all I ever ask of those who enter my world.

The Swastika is the karmic Contact Card. This is the symbol of the path itself—of how and why we choose to walk it and the consequences that result from those choices. Within this energy is the certain echo that what we put out we will get back.

This is also a sign of great mystery and the ability to access and understand great foundational truths. The first of these is that all truths are true—all perspectives are valid, and all that we imagine is somewhere a solid, experiential reality.

The Swastika allows us to entertain alternate routes and probable paths, parallel courses to the one we may have already walked. Yet we must always remember the responsibility that comes with choosing a road that is counter to our trust in the power of light.

This crossroad of decision and discernment is the journey taken by many shamans. However, it has also spawned as many monsters and demons when entered from the dark side of fear.

The center always moves with us wherever we go. Knowing this, we are forever free to remain in our power to choose the path we prefer and not be crushed by the weight of the karmic wheel.

CIRCLES

THE KEY

THE KEY

Though questions will often lead to further
mystery,
they can be solved with application of ability.

All the answers are within; look and you will see
that insight, knowledge, and free will form the
golden key.

I am the magic charm, the secret code, the "open
sesame."
Unlocking doors is what I do; it is my specialty.

I penetrate, investigate, remove obscurity;
no matter how complex the lock, you can
rely on me.
But be forewarned: I insist upon responsibility.

Crack the lock, swing wide the door, set the
secrets free;
to learn the lessons they reveal may take humility
and abiding trust in creation's synchronicity.

Once access has been gained, there flows a
synergy,
accelerating those who seek to be all that
they can be
and imbuing life, wisdom, and pervasive clarity.

For every block and every lock, there is the
perfect key,
forged by blending heart, mind, and soul in
joyous harmony.

I am the symbol that perpetuates self-sufficiency
and provides the tool to integrate in eternal unity.

This card symbolizes the key of knowledge, opening us to the understanding that we already contain the information we need to answer all our questions. We must trust that any fears we discover within us carry needed knowledge that, once integrated, will help us to realize more of our potential as aspects of All That Is.

This card is also a sign that there may be one key fact or ingredient missing from our understanding of the present situation. It encourages us to determine what that might be.

Conversely, The Key may indicate that a piece of knowledge should be kept secret for now, lest its premature revelation cause an imbalance that cannot be easily corrected. This does not mean that we are to be dishonest or furtive, but only that we recognize the importance of proper timing.

Most importantly, the golden key frees us to share who we really are with each other. It inspires us to know that we possess the magical tools to open any door or transform any block in our communication patterns or our ability to discover the treasures in our lives.

SUGGESTED READING

Brown, Courtney, Ph.D. *Cosmic Voyage*. New York: Dutton, 1996.

Carlsberg, Kim. *Beyond My Wildest Dreams*. Santa Fe, N. Mex.: Bear & Company, 1995.

Clow, Barbara Hand. *Chiron: Rainbow Bridge Between the Inner and Outer Planets*. St. Paul: Llewellyn Publications, 1987.

Friedman, Stanton. *Crash at Corona*. New York: Paragon Press, 1992.

Hopkins, Budd. *Intruders*. New York: Random House, 1987.

_____. *Missing Time*. New York: Ballantine Books, 1988.

Howe, Linda Moulton. *Glimpses of Other Realities*. Huntingdon Valley, Penn.: LMH Productions, 1993.

Jacobs, David. *Secret Life*. New York: Simon & Schuster, 1992.

Mack, John. *Abduction: Human Encounters with Aliens*. New York: Macmillan Publishing, 1994.

Noyes, Ralph. *The Crop Circle Enigma*. Bath, U.K.: Gateway Books, 1990.

Rifkin, Jeremy. *Beyond Beef*. New York: Penguin Books, 1993.

Ring, Kenneth, Ph.D. *The Omega Project*. New York: William Morrow & Co., 1992.

Robbins, John. *Diet for a New America*. Hanover, N. Hamp.: Stillpoint Publishing, 1987.

Royal, Lyssa, and Keith Priest. *The Prism of Lyra*. Phoenix, Ariz.: Royal Priest Research Press, 1992.

_____ *Visitors from Within*. Phoenix, Ariz.: Royal Priest
Research Press, 1992.

Sitchin, Zecharia. *The 12th Planet*. Santa Fe, N.Mex.: Bear &
Company, 1990.

Strieber, Whitley. *Communion*. New York: Avon Books,
1987.
_____. *Transformation*. New York: Avon Books, 1988.
_____. *Breakthrough*. New York: HarperCollins Publishers,
1995.

Temple, Robert K.G.. *The Sirius Mystery*. Rochester,
Vermont: Destiny Books, 1987.

Vallee, Jacques. *Dimensions: A Casebook of Alien Contact*. New
York: Ballentine Books, 1988.

Winters, Randolph. *The Pleiadian Mission*. Atwood, Calif.:
The Pleiades Project, Inc., 1994.

ABOUT THE AUTHORS

Kim Carlsberg was born and raised in Kansas City, Missouri. In 1975, at the age of twenty, she moved to Los Angeles, California, where she has resided ever since.

A graduate of Los Angeles Art Center College of Design in commercial photography, Kim is also a member of IATSE, local 659, the motion picture and television camera operators' union.

Kim's career as a fine art and professional celebrity photographer has covered all aspects of the entertainment and music industries. Her credits include photographing former U.S. president, Ronald Reagan.

As a vegetarian, an animal rights activist, and an impassioned enviromentalist, her primary life goals are spiritual and humanitarian.

Darryl Anka was born in Ottawa, Canada, and has lived in Los Angeles for most of his life. He began his career in graphic design, which eventually led to designing special effects for such projects as *Star Trek*, "Babylon 5,"and many other film and television productions.

Darryl is also an internationally acclaimed channel who has conducted interactive workshops and motivational seminars for more than a decade.

He has been active in UFO research since he experienced two close-proximity daylight sightings in Los Angeles in 1973.

Correspondence to the authors should be mailed to:

Kim Carlsberg/Darryl Anka
P.O. Box 8307
Calabasas, CA 91302